The Devil Latch

Sonya Hartnett was born in Melbourne in 1968. Her first novel, *Trouble All the Way*, was published in 1984 when she was fifteen. Since then she has written many novels, most recently *Princes*. Her highly acclaimed novel, *Sleeping Dogs*, was winner of both the 1996 Victorian Premier's Literary Award Shaeffer Pen Prize and the 1996 Miles Franklin Inaugural Kathleen Mitchell Award. It was also named an Honour Book in the 1996 CBC Awards.

By the same author

Trouble all the Way
Sparkle and Nightflower
The Glass House
Sleeping Dogs
Wilful Blue
Black Foxes
Princes

Sonya
HARTNETT

THE DEVIL LATCH

Penguin Books

Penguin Books Australia Ltd
487 Maroondah Highway, PO Box 257
Ringwood, Victoria, 3134, Australia
Penguin Books Ltd
Harmondsworth, Middlesex, England
Viking Penguin, A Division of Penguin Books USA Inc.
375 Hudson Street, New York, New York 10014, USA
Penguin Books Canada Limited
10 Alcorn Avenue, Toronto, Ontario, Canada, M4V 3B2
Penguin Books (N.Z.) Ltd
Cnr Rosedale and Airborne Roads, Albany, Auckland, New Zealand

First published by Penguin Books Australia, 1996
This Penguin edition first published, 1998

10 9 8 7 6 5 4 3 2 1

Typeset in 11.5/17 Sabon by Post Typesetters
Made and printed in Australia by Australian Print Group, Maryborough, Victoria

Cover photograph supplied by International Photo Library
Cover montage by Noel Pennington

National Library of Australia
Cataloguing-in-Publication data:

Hartnett, Sonya, 1968-.
The Devil Latch.

ISBN 0 14 130185 6

I. Title.

A823.3

For John

'It is easy – terribly easy – to shake a man's faith in himself. To take advantage of that, to break a man's spirit, is devil's work.'

George Bernard Shaw, *Candida*

Part one

ON THE ROOF of the garden shed two insects are
fighting to the death. One, a wasp, will win; the other,
a mantis, knows it will lose. A dusty privet shields the
shed from the afternoon sun. It is March, and the
weather is fine. Kitten Latch lies in the shade, scratching idly at the rust in the corrugated iron. In his head,
the demons turn over the things they know.

The Mantis goes by many names: Soothsayer, Mule
Killer, the Devil's Riding Horse. It is a carnivorous
creature: its front, prayerful legs are lined with spikes
to stab and secure the source of its food. The mantis is
the only insect that can turn its head from side to side.
It can be brown, but more usually it is green.

Wasps, too, are carnivorous, although some will also
eat over-ripe vegetable matter. The wasp has a sting,
which it uses to defend itself and to attack its prey.
Wasp venom dissolves red blood cells. A wasp can
choose to sting its prey through the nervous system,
which leaves the victim alive but helpless. Such con-
quests are then transported to the nest to provide food
for the young wasps, which are wholly carnivorous.

Kitten props his chin on his hands. The wasp is a
swarming insect, and it swarms over the mantis. Its

3 ⟶

assault remains urgent even after the mantis has weakened and ceased to defend itself, and Kitten feels the beat of teardrop wings against his face, hears the furious buzz. He hears, too, the noises coming from the house next door, but he does not bother to look up. The wasp begins to disassemble the mantis before the defeated is dead.

A wasp likes warm weather and hates the rain. It is also surprisingly finicky in its tastes. If its meal is a blowfly, it will sever the head, wings and legs and leave them where they lie, flying off with only the chubby torso. Kitten is interested and surprised, then, when the wasp clips through the mantis's narrow waist and hoists the front half of the body into the air, taking what he had expected it to discard. Do the wings and legs and head of a mantis taste different, then, from those of a fly? The remaining half writhes briefly, showing the pale belly to the sky. The wasp, clumsy with its angular load, is not difficult for Kitten to catch and crush under his hand. Predator and prey are left as one, against the peeling paint.

Kitten yawns and rubs at his eyes. In his head the demons are restless and kick at their confines, like cramped twins in a womb. They are, in fact, twins, although the colour of one is black, the other blazing red. They are naked in there, but armed with sharp teeth and the vilest of tempers. The arrival of the people next door has made them curious, and angry, so they twist and twist and twist, giving Kitten no peace.

He sits up, cleans his hand of the wasp remains, and leaps from the roof of the garden shed.

Agatha is in the kitchen, standing at the sink. From here she has watched Kitten through the window, although she could not see what had held his interest so long. She watches him cross the garden, keeping always to the path, sees him wipe his feet against the mat and step into the house. She has known him since he was little, and she takes care of him, as she takes care of Kitten's grandfather, Paul. She offers him a cup of tea, but he does not even glance at her. He is making for his grandfather's bedroom and she takes the kettle from the stove, extinguishes the flame.

The grandfather swivels his eyes when Kitten enters the room. Kitten crosses the floor and pulls the curtains, and the room is filled with the white afternoon light. The old man gags and splutters and screws shut his eyes; he cannot turn his head away, for the creeping stiffness has recently reached his neck. He is hardening, like a plant, from the roots up.

Kitten nods at the view, which his grandfather can not see. 'We have,' he says, 'new neighbours. Isn't that nice?'

The old man makes a crackling noise in his throat, and Kitten casts him a quick and benevolent smile. 'They've been shifting in all day,' he says, and returns his gaze to the front garden. 'A young man, and a young woman. Living in sin, I suppose.'

His grandfather makes a barking sound; not, Kitten

knows, the sound for old-fashioned beliefs, or the sound for old-fashioned beliefs being mocked, but the sound that is all that remains of the old man's once formidable rage. He wants to protest Kitten's invasion of the room, the drawing of the curtains, the letting in of the light. Kitten smiles vaguely, as if he understands nothing of this, and leans his weight against the sill.

'They have brought a lot of things with them,' he explains. 'They have boxes and boxes. They have a cat, and the cat was also in a box. It wasn't a good box, and the cat escaped. It is a grey cat, and it moved very fast. Ptolemy, is what its name is: the girl called, Ptolemy! Ptolemy! as she ran after it.'

He glances over his shoulder, to make sure the old man is listening. His grandfather's body is an angular narrow ridge under the covers of the bed. He is watching Kitten closely, and his clenched teeth are showing. In the sunlight his lips glisten damply and the dust shows itself on the furniture. Kitten looks beyond the window.

'The cat ran across the garden, and leaped up and over the fence. It was in our garden then, but it did not know it, it simply ran and ran. And it was running for our back fence, running for its life, and that's when it saw Cocky, and Cocky saw it. And Cocky screeched – did you hear him? – and the cat stopped in its tracks, and fuzzed itself up. Perhaps it has never seen a thing such as Cocky: he certainly is a sight.'

The old man is listening now, and his fury at his

grandson has died down, for Cocky is the only thing he loves, and he concentrates his energy into hearing the story.

'Cat looks at Cocky, Cocky looks at cat. Ptolemy, a king, an idiot cat.'

Kitten sighs and shrugs, as if he has grown bored with telling the tale. He has big eyes that are coloured a foolish blue, and he turns and blinks them at his grandfather. The old man waits, and waits longer, and finally he cannot stand the sight and is moved to hiss, 'Bastard.'

The twins in Kitten's head open their eyes.

'Bastard. Bastard.'

'What is that you're saying, Pauly?'

'Vicious bastard,' spits Paul Latch.

Kitten laughs; he takes a cigarette from his pocket and lights it. 'You have such a very black heart,' he says. The old man does not realise that each hateful word makes Kitten stronger. Kitten blows smoke across the room, and looks again out the window.

'And then,' he says, 'the girl climbed the fence. She climbed it and jumped to the ground and looked around our garden. Ptolemy! she whispered: Ptolemy, come here! She kept very low to the earth, as if that would hide her, and she moved very slowly, as if this is what cat preferred. But cat did not hear her: cat was looking at Cocky. So she was able to pick cat up and carry him away, stroking his head, calling him bad. All this I saw, but she did not see me. I know what she is called: she is

Aimee. The young man is Curtis. I have watched them all day. I know what their furniture looks like, and I know the clothes they wear. I know the paintings that will hang on their walls, and the plates from which they'll eat their meals. I know their house better than they do: I know the boards that creak and the tiles that are loose, I know how tightly to turn off the taps. I know each flower in their garden and each stone in their driveway. I know the shape and size of the rooms, and I know the windows that will let you in, and out.'

Kitten stops, and contemplates the ash gathered at the tip of his cigarette. The old man is eyeing him, but his gaze soon falls to what his grandchild sees. The ash clings delicately to the red coal, held together by its own design. Kitten looks at the carpet on which the ash will drop, holding its cylindrical shape all the way down until the shattering instant when it hits the floor. It will need only one dab with his bare toes to make it impossible to clean away. The old man will never see it, but his knowledge of the dirty patch will eat at him. Paul Latch's eyes are bulging. Inside Kitten's head, the demons turn and turn.

Kitten lets the moment hold. Then he opens his free hand and taps the ash into his palm. 'Do you know what I think?' he asks his grandfather. 'I think our Ptolemy will be back.'

A soft moaning comes from the old man. In his bed he lies prone, he will never move, but the sound says everything he would like to do, tells everything he remembers he could do, how he longs to crush Kitten like a bug. Kitten considers him for a moment, letting the cigarette burn. Then he walks away from the window and stops beside the bed, and stares down at his grandfather.

'There's no cause to whimper,' he says. 'You needn't think these new people will distract me. I will never leave you. I am your familiar: I'm here to help.'

'Kitten,' says Agatha, and Kitten lifts his head. To look at him, caught by surprise as he is, she can scarcely believe in his wicked soul. She has stood beyond the doorway and heard every taunting thing he has said, but the face he lifts to her is that of an angel, with the softest whitest locks, the unflawed flesh of a child, an expression that is guileless. But is not beauty the perfect disguise? Why, she thinks, would a devil be anything but beautiful?

'Kitten,' she says sharply, being hard on him. 'Kitten, you know you're not to smoke in here. Take it out. Take yourself out into the nice day.'

He looks contrite and slinks from the room, batting his lashes as he passes her. When she hears him swing the fly-screen she goes to the bed and fusses with the covers although they need no adjusting, for Paul makes no move to disturb them. The old man says nothing and does not look at her. They are both thinking: a familiar is a creature that attends the evil.

The houses in this street are dark and heavy, for they were built in dark and heavy times, when eldest sons were fighting wars. They are built low and many are kept neat by widows and widowers, for it is a neighbourhood where death creeps about in the night, gently dispatching the elderly occupants. The gardens are large and unadventurous: here and there is a failed native garden, but most of the plants are English trees and shrubs. The neighbours know each other and have done so for years, but they do not collect on corners to chat: their friendliness rarely extends beyond a genial nod of the head and sympathetic acknowledgments of health and weather. Small pets are kept here, canaries and terriers and world-weary felines: anything bigger can be such a nuisance. There is little noise apart from bird calls and the occasional visiting, grizzling grandchild. Cars go up and down the street slowly, heading for somewhere else. This is suburbia, sturdy, wealthy, established. When the house beside the Latches' went up for rent, the tone of the area threatened to take a dive. Young people do not want to live here, and few do, but the residents feared the descent of hoodlums, drug addicts, and loud music. Kitten Latch was not the only one who watched as Aimee and Curtis shifted in. Aimee feels the eyes upon her as she moves from the garden to the house. She struggles alone with their possessions: her brother has taken the trailer and gone home, too busy to carry the luggage further than the front fence, and Curtis has retreated to the spare room, to unpack his treasured computers.

Ptolemy is scratching and yowling from behind the

bedroom door and eventually she frees him and hugs him, although this is something he hates. She drops into an armchair and puts her face in his coat, and peers at the room from under her brow. This house reminds her of her own grandmother's house, for they are all of the same ilk, the floral wallpaper, the dark-stained wood, the chillness that resists the warmest days, and she wonders if the owner of this place, like her grandmother, has passed on to another world. In a cupboard she has found a vinyl travelbag emblazoned with the logo of an airline that no longer exists.

This is the first time she has moved out from home. She would have preferred to take a terrace house close to the city, where there are shops, neon lights and the spirit of youth, but Curtis said the rent was cheaper here, and the streets are quieter, and they need to save their money, and he needs peace to work. And she agreed to that, because that is what she does.

Aimee puts the cat down and walks through the house, to the rear garden. Here there is a pond with-out water, and fuchsias plagued by whitefly. She lives, now, in a cold house with low rent in a street that is silent, but she is with Curtis, her beloved, and that is what is important. Tonight they will sleep in a place that is their own, and the knowledge fills her with a greedy happiness. Taking a house, living with your boyfriend: this is life. This is what living is about. She is on the way to living life as it is meant to be lived. She feels as if she has finally become real.

The garden must have been tended once, for there are many plants and the remains of a vegetable patch, but everything has been overrun with weeds which she supposes must be pulled. When she looks around she sees it is really quite a pretty place, with a seat below the elm, and the pond which can be repaired, and if she gets a book from the library she could make the vegetables grow again. She walks about with bare feet: there are no burrs in the grass. The fence is falling down in sections, and the pointed foliage of the plant beyond the fence pokes through, waving to attract her attention. She goes to it, wraps her palms around the beckoning leaves, and peeks through the gap in the palings. She cannot see clearly the yard beyond, but she sees the cage that contains the bird that brought Ptolemy to a halt, and she hears the creature scrabbling around inside. The bird is a cockatoo, and is almost naked of feathers. When she'd collected the thunderstruck Ptolemy the bird had turned its head to look at her, and the skin around its eyeball was red and traced with a thousand wrinkles, and the tunnel of the ear had turned black within the skull.

For no reason she looks up and around, and sees the young man watching her. From high up on a tree branch he watches her, lazing like a lynx. Startled, Aimee steps back. 'Hello,' she says, not certain what to say.

For a moment she thinks he will not reply, but then he says, 'Hello.'

His white hair makes it hard for him to hide, but she thinks he is not bothering to hide, that he wanted to be seen. 'That's a long way up,' she says. 'You'd better be careful.'

'Not as careful as you need to be,' he calmly replies.

And of course she feels the first qualm then, the twitch of oddness. She glances around but there is nowhere to go, no retreat that wouldn't seem impolite. 'We've just shifted in,' she explains, for there's nothing else to say.

'Yes, I know.'

'My name is Aimee.'

He nods, rubbing his cheek against the branch.

'I'm living here . . . with my boyfriend.'

He doesn't bother to nod again. He scans her garden and the rooftop of her house. 'Curtis is inside, playing with his computers,' she says. 'That's all he does, play with his computers.'

'Is that so?' asks the boy in the tree.

'He doesn't play – he works, I guess. All the time, he works on his computers.' She gives a thin laugh, wondering why she's volunteering this information. She babbles, when she's nervous.

'That must be very boring for you,' he says. 'How very boring that must be.'

'Sometimes,' she admits.

'If you like, tomorrow I can take you to a place that you won't find boring.'

Aimee hesitates. 'Oh,' she says, 'I don't know –'

'You have a bicycle?'

'. . . Curtis does.'

'You could borrow it.'

'I could, but – we've just shifted in, and –'

He tosses his head, as if to avoid the sound of her excuses, as if her trepidation is an insulting, tedious thing. 'It's well worth seeing,' he says. 'I shouldn't take you there otherwise.'

Aimee opens her mouth and says nothing. High up, the air gusts, and billows the boy's white hair around his face. The breeze brings to him the scent of her resignation.

'Good,' he says. 'Tomorrow. Shall I knock on your door?'

She thinks that Curtis might find this upsetting, to have a strange young man come asking for her at their door. 'No,' she says. 'No . . . I'll come and get you.'

'Don't forget.'

'No . . .'

'Goodbye, then,' he says.

Aimee staggers back, so evidently dismissed. She glances at him once more, and he looks placidly back at her. She turns for the house and he asks, 'Don't you want to know what you must be careful of?'

She lifts her face to him again, feeling dizzy.

'That plant you were touching,' says Kitten. 'That's an oleander, and poisonous. Wash your hands.'

AT THE SWAMP he tells her this story about himself: when he was a boy his father took him to a house in the country, and it seemed very far away. With them went a woman who was not his mother, Kitten guessed, because she did not know his name, but she treated him kindly and bought him a colouring book and a packet of textas. He remembers that the colours went through the pages of the book, ruining the picture on the other side. He had not wanted to go and was fretful about the prospect but his grandmother wanted him to go, had explained the briefness of a weekend and how nice the days away would be for him. Finally, she told him he had to go, to escape his grandfather for a time. So, not happy, he went.

He'd never seen this country house before. All he remembers of it now is the fields of grass that could swallow a small boy whole, and the fascinating, terrifying outside toilet. The toilet was a plank of wood with a circle cut out of it and, beneath this, a pitch black tunnel that ran away into invisibility. This tunnel could harbour some monster of slime that was capable of reaching a thin muscular arm around a boy and dragging him, grey with terror, into the reeking depths. Kitten visited this place more often than was necessary, entranced, gleefully horrified.

Night had fallen when his father and the woman began to fight. Kitten was sitting on the floor with his colouring book when the yelling words came through the wall and he looked up, lifting his pen. He felt his vulnerability, then, alone in a strange room, a little boy marooned with people he did not know, people who would scream at each other and not care if he heard and was afraid. He was only six.

The argument is about pyjamas. Kitten has forgotten to bring his pyjamas. The weight of his accidental crime presses him to the floor as the voices boom through the house. The woman is saying it does not matter, forget it, forget she said a damn thing, but the father says he is going back to get the pyjamas and why must she make such a bloody hysterical fuss about everything, he's sick of her, sick of everything, he's driving back through the night and the rain to get the fucking pyjamas.

'No!' the woman howls, in agony. 'It's raining, you've been drinking, don't be a fool, you're being a fool!' But the father doesn't answer, he thumps down the hall, slams the front door, drives away. The house, then, is quiet. Kitten holds his breath. The rocking silence his father leaves behind is just as bad as the noise. He is alone in a strange house with a strange woman, and now the woman is weeping. Kitten hesitates a moment, and lays down his colouring pen.

The woman is in the big bedroom. Clothes and things are flung untidily on the floor. She does not hear Kitten creep up behind her, but she feels him tug at the hem of her dress. 'Don't cry,' he says. 'Daddy will be all right, I'm sure he'll be all –'

The woman wheels around. With her crumpled dress and tear-washed makeup she is a monster with thin arms.

'Get out!' she roars at him. 'Get out get out get out get out!'

And in that awful moment, when he stood stricken with shock and the woman despised him, he learned that innocence is the thing of fools. A woman could kill a child, a man is a beast of stomping fury. In that moment he changed forever, he knew he'd never feel that stinging loss again, and the twins came to him, and opened their eyes. The twins would watch the world for him, guard him, arm him, be his secret defence. With time they would grow powerful, and tell him the things he could do.

Kitten snaps a twig and looks at Aimee. He does not mention the twins. 'Get out,' he repeats. 'Get out, get out, get out.'

Aimee is staring at him. 'My God,' she says, and gives an awkward laugh. 'What happened then?'

Kitten shrugs. 'Then, she realised what she had done. I think she saw the badness of the thing she had done. And she said she was sorry. She said she was not angry at me. I found it difficult, to forgive her.'

'You were only a child. Children don't understand.'

'But I did understand,' corrects Kitten Latch. 'I understood. I knew about anger. I was used to the anger of my grandfather. His anger was always pointed, like a pin. He'd skewer you with it. But I thought he was different, that my grandmother was telling the truth when she said he was strange and no others were like him. The woman made me see that my grandmother was wrong.'

'Your father, too. Yelling like that.'

'Yes. It became clear to me that some are dangerous, and the rest are vulnerable.'

He had known, then, in his sudden and clear discernment of the situation, that he was not of the vulnerable. He had realised, then, his purpose: he was not to let evil escape unscathed. The twins stretched in their tight confines, shredding their cauls with bladed fingers, touching their shark teeth with the tips of blunt tongues. They were born with voices: whispers of their dreadful chatter hummed softly in his ears. He had stepped away from the woman, but before his foot found the floor he had lost his fear of her. He would not forgive her because he knew he did not have to, he knew his small frame was bigger, stronger, than she, he had seen through her like glass.

He has grown bored with telling the story, and knows it is dangerous to explain too much. The twins are growling in his head: they do not like it when he talks of how things are for him. But Aimee asks, 'So what happened? Did your father come back?'

'Of course he came back,' Kitten replies. 'He brought the pyjamas. He looked like a fool. I saw him only one more time, a few years after, but he bored me then, and he was still a fool.'

'That's a terrible thing to happen to a child, Kitten. That's a terrible story.'

'I am pleased you appreciate it.'

'I feel sorry for the little boy you must have been, standing there alone, scared.'

He looks at her oddly, as if her compassion unsettles him. Aimee feels his reticence, and lets the subject drop. Her family is a happy one, and it always saddens her to find that not all families are the same. She looks around the murky swamp: her legs are tired from the bike ride but there is nowhere, on the muddy banks, for her to sit and rest. The swamp is surrounded by trees, and trees rise out of the swamp itself, trees that must look like Kitten's imagined monster in the tunnel for their limbs are long and spindly, their trunks are coated with slime. The water is grim and oily and herons step through the shallows, driving their dagger beaks into the mud. Kitten knows this place well, but not many others do. It is close to the freeway but it is quiet, and she keeps her voice low. Nearby is a civilised walking track, but they had dragged their bicycles through scrub and thistles to get here, and the only footprints around them are their own.

'Is it deep?' she asks. 'Is the swamp deep?'

'Not now. When it rains, it will be deep.'

Aimee looks up to the sky. It is blue, it's not going to rain.

'So you are living with Curtis,' states Kitten, and snaps another twig from the tree.

'Yes,' she says. 'It's like . . . a real thing. Something to say that . . . my life is going the way it is meant to go.'

Kitten looks at her. 'Are you to marry him, and have his children, is that the way your life is meant to go?'

'I hope so.'

Kitten sighs. 'How idiotic that sounds to me.'

'Not everyone wants a different life,' she says, defensive. 'What is wrong with wanting what I want?'

'Nothing.'

'And what do you want?'

'Nothing,' he repeats, and lights a cigarette. 'I was unaware that people are supposed to want anything at all.'

Aimee hesitates, and her shoulders fall. 'It is what I want,' she says. 'We shouldn't all try to be remarkable. I'm not very clever. Only my mum and dad and Curtis think I am special. Curtis is clever enough for both of us. He's the one who can live the remarkable life. He works with computers. He's going to make computers even more important than they already are. He's got a big plan.'

'What if everyone does not want computers to be a thing of great importance? Why does Curtis inflict his big plans upon others who have done him no harm?'

'He's not harming them, he's helping them –'

'I should like to meet your Curtis one day,' Kitten says. 'Curtis, with his computers.'

'Please don't be unkind about him. He is good to me.'

'You are his pet, as the cat is yours. You are a pretty but dim little bauble in his life. Not so pretty that you cannot cart furniture; dim enough to be banished to wander the garden while he works. You are his toy and his slave.'

Aimee glares at him. Kitten stands smoking his cigarette, so coolly composed she can scarcely believe he's spoken the astonishing words. She thinks she should be spirited and stalk away but her heart's not in the idea, and she doesn't make a move. From him comes a serenity that makes her annoyance seem ridiculous and rude. 'The cat belongs to Curtis,' she says lamely, and Kitten gives a charming laugh. He unnerves and agitates her but, strange, she likes him, as if she's compelled to do so.

'How old are you?' she asks, and he smiles.

'How old do I seem?'

She looks at him. His hair is snowy, his eyes are blue. His face is thin and without lines: he is flawless like a flower, beautiful like an animal. She says, 'You look about eighteen years old.'

'I think,' he tells her, 'that it is closer to eighteen thousand.'

She laughs, feeling playful, and asks him, 'How old do you think I am?'

'You are twenty,' he replies, and her smile broadens, because he is right. 'Will you come home for tea?'

She does not want to, but she thinks she owes him something after he has shown her the swamp, his special place. They ride back together through the empty streets. She drops her bike into the grass of his front garden and follows him into his house. It is a house that has held the same people for many years, and it has been made to suit them. The furniture in the lounge is heavy and the shape of the sitters has been left behind in the cushions. There are books and side-boards and tiny things: a pretty clock, silver candle-sticks, the better porcelain locked up behind glass. Around the walls, landscapes are hung from stretches of wire. The carpet is durable, and clean except for the dusty corners. The television is draped with a plastic cover. A vase props up three wilted roses. The elderly inhabitants are evident here, but Aimee sees no signs of a young man. The videos, she notes, are operas.

'Agatha, Agatha, this is Aimee. We must give her something to eat.' He says this to an older woman who is wiping the kitchen table. Aimee thinks this must be his grandmother but Kitten explains, 'This is Agatha Latch, my great-aunt.'

'Hello,' says Aimee. The woman greets her cour-teously, and puts the kettle on the stove. She moves slowly; her hands are arthritic and swollen; how used

Kitten must be, Aimee thinks, to this world where nothing can be done quickly, and infirmity is always something to be considered. How often must his young heart be nettled by the ponderousness that is age? He is taking down cups and pouring out biscuits while the old woman labours with the matchbox.

'You've just moved in next door, haven't you?'

'That's right –'

'Planning to stay long?'

'Oh,' says Aimee, 'I don't know.'

'Do you have any friends living nearby? Anyone besides your beau?'

'No,' says Aimee, 'not really. Most of my friends are people Curtis knew before I did. They're his friends, mostly. I like them, though, they're nice to me. I don't see any of the people I went to school with, any more. You know – that happens. You just – lose touch.'

The older woman nods, sympathetic. 'It's a shame.'

'I'll make the tea, Agatha,' Kitten says suddenly. Agatha drops her hands, backs away from the stove.

'What about your family? Do you have brothers and sisters? Do they live close?'

'I've got a brother, an elder brother. There's him and me and Mum and Dad. They live on the other side of the city. I haven't got a car: it takes me ages to get there on public transport.'

Agatha twists her apron string. 'You're a bit isolated, then . . .'

'Well, I've met Kitten, and I've only been here one day.'

'Yes,' says Kitten, 'she's friends with me. She won't be alone.'

Agatha nods; she has a broad, round face, and her grey hair is neatly done. 'That's nice,' she says. 'You'd best watch out for him, though: he's full of mischief. Aren't you, Kitten?'

'I'll make the tea, Agatha,' he repeats. He is frowning at her and the old woman stares back at him for a moment, and pouts her lip. This makes Aimee laugh, but Kitten's look is black.

'Stop trying to be funny,' he says. 'Go in the other room and leave us alone. Aimee doesn't want to answer your silly questions.'

Agatha gives Aimee a wan smile. 'He's bossy,' she says, and shuffles from the room. Kitten looks at Aimee.

'She needs to be kept under control,' he says.

'Old people like to ask questions. I don't mind.'

'But I mind,' Kitten replies. 'I mind, and she knows it.'

When she's drunk her tea and eaten a biscuit he lets her leave without asking when they might meet again. She goes home feeling content with the day, and meets Curtis in the hall. 'What were you doing in the house next door?' he asks. 'I saw the bike in the yard.'

His tone makes her unusually cross. 'Does everyone watch everything in this street?' she yelps, and pushes roughly past him. 'You're allowed to stay hidden in your study all day, and I'm not allowed to do or see a single thing, is that how it's meant to be?'

She never raises her voice to him, and he is startled. He has his cat curled in his arms and he squeezes the soft body, making Ptolemy twitch his tail.

'They invited me in for tea and I couldn't refuse, could I? You work all day and all night, I didn't think you'd miss me.'

'I'm trying to start a career, Aimee –'

'Fine,' she says. 'And in the meantime there's nothing for me to do.'

'I'm not angry at you,' he says soothingly, as if to a hysterical animal. 'Look, the sun is out. Why don't you make a pot of coffee and we'll take it outside, to the garden?'

She looks at him, holding his cat. 'I'm not your toy, or your slave,' she says. 'Make it yourself.'

Kitten goes out into the garden, to where Cocky sits in his cage. The bird knows him and steps onto Kitten's wrist when he puts his hand through the door. He transfers the bird to his shoulder and the creature nuzzles against his ear, tugs at hanks of his hair. Kitten hears its heartbeat through the thin naked skin. The bird flaps its tattered wings as Kitten walks back to the house, and the points of the broad claws grip against his bones.

He takes the bird into his grandfather's room, and hauls back the curtains.

'Look who I've brought to visit you,' he tells the old man, who is squinting and snorting air. 'I'm in such a

25 ⟫

good mood today that I've brought in your little plucked friend.'

He detaches Cocky from his shoulder and sits the bird on the bedstead. Paul Latch must peer down the humped length of his body to see it.

'I'll put the cover over his cage, later, because I think it's going to rain. Don't you think so? Look out the window, Paul. Don't you?'

His grandfather darts his eyes at the window. He does not wish to look, he never wants to do anything Kitten tells him to do, but he is a man used to giving his opinion even now, when he can scarcely form his words. Kitten doesn't wait for an answer: 'I do,' he says. 'I know it will rain. Can't let Cocky get wet.'

The bird is bobbing its head, rippling the snake-skinned throat. Paul Latch watches it, smiles a miserable smile. Kitten yawns, and Paul shifts his gaze to him. He is surprised when his grandson draws the curtains and leaves the room. And then he is suspicious, thinking he is being lulled, and the devil will return at the very moment Paul believes himself to be safe.

The door remains closed for long minutes. The bird nibbles quietly at its tongue. Somewhere in the house there is a radio playing the songs Agatha likes, old tunes that take her back to her youth. He imagines how she must dream of her dead husband. Paul never dreams of his dead wife. His wife's name was Gloria and from the moment she died she has been far from him, has never returned, not even in his sleep. It is as if she's relieved to be gone. His memories of her are still-lifes from photographs, something anyone can see.

Still, the door stays closed. If it opens he thinks he will howl like a child. The devil uses suspense, it is one of the favourite weapons, and one of the worst. He said he was in a good mood and Paul suspects there's a new trick hidden there, for it's a line Kitten has never used before.

But, the door stays closed. Paul Latch, who is nothing but a hard old weight in his bed, wants to thrash and scream. He is helpless and vulnerable here, he, who had been a man of power. They had cowered respectfully before him, his wife, his idiot son, the people he employed. Thirty years ago he expressed a whim to own a cockatoo and a minion scurrying about on the bottom rung of his company went out and caught him one, from the wild.

Now, he lives in fear of a closed door.

Paul Latch is seventy years old. He was fifty-seven years old when he first began to stiffen. The company he had established when a young man was large and prosperous by that time, but he and Gloria still lived in the modest house where they had lived their entire married life, where they'd raised their craven son. Paul saw no reason to shift into larger premises simply because he could afford to do so, and he did not judge Gloria capable of running a bigger house.

The stiffening had begun with faint, irritating tingles in his ankles. He'd refused to see a doctor. And the tingling went away, as he had told Gloria it would. It left behind something worse, a toughening of the skin, a thickening in the muscles. Like water sucked up by a tree, the thickening reached his calves, and then his knees. It travelled slowly but with determination. He never lost feeling: he simply ceased to be able to move. His joints, locked in the thickening, would not bend.

He went to the doctors and endured their tests. When they said they could not stop the spread of this affliction, he called them fools. At home, he cried.

It was impossible to go to work in a wheeled chair, his legs stuck out ridiculously before him. For as long as he could he worked from home. It was not in him to retire.

He worked from nine to five in the dining room, his papers spread about the table, with exactly forty-five minutes break for lunch. Within a year the thickening had banded around his hips and gripped the base of his spine. Like a bow his body arched, then, painful, and undignified. Inevitably, he lay down.

The door is still closed, and Paul begins to breathe again. The cockatoo plumps out its few feathers and stares at him. He never taught the bird to talk and would not let anyone else do so. He did not want it looking a fool, mindlessly repeating whatever it was told. The door closed, Paul gurgles to the animal under his breath, softly, so if the devil is listening beyond the wall he may not hear. The old man never forgets that the stiffening, wasting destruction of his body began not long after Kitten Latch was dumped at his door.

EVERY DAY THAT week a misty rain falls, never
heavy enough to soak anything through, falling quietly
and inconspicuously as if embarrassed to be there at
all. Aimee goes to work each morning, catching a tram
and sitting on dampened seats, filing and typing and
doing as she is told. In the cool evenings she walks
home from the tram stop and looks at each house as
she passes by, familiarising herself with the things that
surround her now. Her step quickens as she closes in
on Kitten's home, hoping to see him in his garden or
fishing his pocket for his keys, but he is never there.
Five days pass and she does not see him. Why this dis-
appoints her she does not know, yet so it is: she has a
sense of having been cast aside. Has she done something wrong? Has she bored him? She feels a desperate
need to restore a friendship that scarcely exists at all.

'What are you looking for?' Curtis asks her, when
she stands at the window with the venetian slats
propped apart, and every time Aimee answers him,
'Nothing.'

Finally, on Friday evening, she goes to his door. She
goes up the small steps and knocks timidly on the door,
and it is opened by Kitten himself. He is taller than she

and looks down at her from his height: he does not seem surprised to see her. 'Oh, hello,' he says, as if he saw her every day.

She feels nervous, as the rejected always do. She stumbles over what she wants to say to him, which is to request he come and visit her, to see the place where she lives, to understand the way her life is, all this couched in an invitation for coffee.

'Certainly,' he says, and steps out of the house.

Skirting their dividing fence she feels insanely happy, as if she has captured some fantastic beast.

Curtis is home from work and when they are introduced he says to Kitten, 'You're Aimee's friend from next door, are you?'

'That's right,' replies Kitten, and Aimee is proud.

'You invited her over for tea.'

'Indeed. I have also shown her the local landmarks worth seeing. We must show them to you too, one day.'

'I can't imagine there's anything to see around here. The place is full of old ladies walking midget dogs.'

'It's not, though,' says Aimee. 'You should see it, Curtis, there's this amazing –'

'Aimee,' says Kitten, 'don't spoil it for him.'

Aimee nods agreeably, and Curtis looks at their visitor. 'Kitten,' he states. 'Is that your real name?'

'Possibly,' says Kitten.

Curtis waits for him to add something more, but when Kitten remains silent he fumbles and asks, 'Would you like a beer?'

'No, thank you. I've come for coffee.'

'I'll have a beer,' Curtis tells Aimee, who is going to the kitchen.

Kitten gazes around the lounge room. He has been in this room many times, when it has been occupied and empty, and he knows it well. The new inhabitants do not have enough possessions to make it look very different from the way it has always been. There are only two armchairs and if he takes one it means Aimee must stand, for Curtis seems disinclined to move from where he slouches, his grey cat stretched at his feet. Kitten feels the young man's awkwardness at his presence in the room, and the demon twins smile in his head. Aimee must have invited him on her own, not bothering to ask if her boyfriend cared.

Curtis is dark-haired and solid, with a face that is dull. Kitten knows much about him simply from looking, and he is not surprised when Curtis asks him, 'So, what do you do?'

'What do I do?' Kitten repeats. He has stopped before the fireplace and rests an elbow on the mantel. 'Do you mean, what do I do for a living?'

Curtis seems baffled by this response. He has used the line with many people and never had to explain what he meant.

'I am rather more interested in what you do,' Kitten continues. 'Aimee tells me you work with computers.'

'I'm working for a company at the moment, but only until I've got the finances to set up my own business. I'm developing new software. It's going to be quite revolutionary.'

'Another revolution. How nice.'

'You know a bit about computers, do you?'

'No, I don't. Actually, I dislike computers. I dislike the way they have intruded into this world without asking the least permission.'

'Better learn to live with it, buddy,' says Curtis. He sits up straighter in his seat, thinking he has the advantage here. 'There's no place for anyone who can't use a computer.'

'That makes me,' says Kitten, 'very sad indeed.'

Aimee returns, carrying two cups of coffee. She dashes back to the kitchen to get Curtis a can of beer. To Kitten she says, 'I made it white, without sugar. Is that how you like it?'

'It is. Thank you.'

Aimee smiles merrily. He waves her towards the vacant seat and she sits down, lifting her small face to him. 'Where have you been all week?' she asks. 'What have you been doing?'

'We were just talking about what Curtis is doing.'

'It's a bit complicated, if you don't know anything about the field. Basically, I work in communications.'

'Everything's going to seem old-fashioned in a few years,' Aimee says proudly. 'Books and letters and radio and television and telephones. All of it. We'll wonder how we lived like we do.'

Kitten lifts an eyebrow. Curtis swigs from his beer.

'Soon,' he says, 'you'll never need to leave your house.'

'What a curious prospect,' muses Kitten. 'Will the world revert to jungle, if no one ever leaves their house? Maybe there is some accidental virtue in this grand scheme after all.'

'You don't think there's any virtue in being able to see and talk to someone on the other side of the globe, with just a computer screen in between?'

'None I can think of. Isn't it better that the world remains a big place? Why do you want to squeeze ocean and land and distance and time into meaninglessness? It seems to me a hollow victory, defeating the vastness of the planet.'

'The vastness of the planet has never been a good thing. There'll be a lot less bad stuff happening the moment everyone knows what everyone else is doing and thinking and saying.'

Kitten laughs lazily. 'You are a crusader for good? My, my. You are a fool, if you think wickedness is that easy to eradicate. I think that is the most stupid thing I have ever heard.'

Curtis is becoming irritated. He stares at the snowy-haired young man lounging before his fireplace, and slurps aggressively from his beer. Even the cat finds the visitor offensive and stalks, tail swinging, into another room.

'If you watch television or use a telephone or listen to the radio you're already participating in the squeezing of your precious globe,' Curtis says.

Kitten nods. 'My aunt listens to the radio.'

'You talk as if you come from another century. All this was happening years before you or I came along.'

'Yes, but I wonder if that makes any difference at all.'

'Live in your own little box, if you like, and ignore the thing, but it's only you who'll pay the price.'

'It seems to me that those who share your enthusiasm shall be the ones living in the little boxes. The rest will have the jungle. I think I know which I would prefer.'

Aimee chuckles. 'It will bring us back to the start of time,' she says. 'The cavemen will overthrow the box-people and club every computer to death.'

Curtis looks at her as if at a traitor; Kitten smiles, and the twins are hooting like drains. After a moment Curtis asks, 'So anyway, what do you do?'

A look of boredom crosses Kitten's face, and he shifts his gaze from Aimee to Curtis. 'Are you asking if I am employed or not? I suppose the answer is no. Yes, I suppose the answer is no.'

'You suppose?'

'What I do, I do for love.'

Curtis does not quite understand. 'If you're on the dole, say so,' he prompts. 'How do you get the money to live?'

'I do not need money to live,' Kitten replies, and Curtis gives an ugly laugh.

'What are you?' he asks. 'A fucking hippy or something? One of those New Age dickheads? You don't need money to live: don't give me that bullshit.'

'You find it difficult to believe?'

'I find it a load of bollocks, is what I find it. Wake up, kitty-cat: the world's not that sort of place. It's never been that sort of place. You've got to fight your way through it, and fight all the bastards who'll be stepping in your way. Your responsibility is to yourself in this world, and anyone who's a failure has only themselves to blame.'

Kitten blinks at him. In his head the twins drum their heels, convulsed with laughter.

'Is this true?' he asks. 'Can what you say really be true?'

'Take my word for it, buddy,' answers Curtis. 'Get off your arse and do something.'

'Curtis,' says Kitten Latch, 'I think I will.'

He drinks the rest of his cooling coffee, and looks around the room. 'What you've done with this place is very pretty,' he says.

Aimee has grown tense, listening to Curtis rave. She is afraid Kitten is upset, and relieved to see he is not. 'We don't have very much,' she says. 'Everything looks a bit sparse.'

'We have everything we need,' says Curtis, gruffly.

'We need a couch,' Aimee bites back. 'One day we might get one.'

Kitten nods. 'Well,' he sighs, 'I must go. Thank you for inviting me in.'

She sees him to the door, and outside in the darkness he turns to her. She looks up at him, suddenly shy, wanting to say something to keep him close. 'I'm sorry Curtis was so rude,' she says.

'It was entertaining.'

'Do you really hate computers?'

'I was interested in what Curtis would say if I did.'

'You were teasing him!' She laughs. 'You were entertaining yourself!'

He smiles; his devil's teeth glitter.

'Are you to have another boring weekend,' he asks, 'while Curtis wallows in ambition?'

'No,' Aimee replies. 'He said that tomorrow he will take me out.'

'I see. And Sunday? Are you being taken out on Sunday?'

'. . . No.'

Kitten nods. 'Then on Sunday you must come to visit me. Come at one o'clock, and Agatha will cook a roast.'

Promptly at one she knocks on Kitten's door, and it is opened by Agatha. 'Kitten's not here, sweetheart,' she says. 'He's been gone since early this morning.'

'He said he would be here,' Aimee says, reddening. 'He invited me for lunch.'

'Did he? Then he'll probably be back very soon. Come in.'

Agatha holds the door open for her, and Aimee steps into the house. She follows the woman to the kitchen, where Agatha says, 'I'm glad you've come. Every Sunday

I cook a roast, and so much of it goes to waste. Kitten and his grandfather eat like sparrows. I really should stop bothering, I know, but Mr Latch likes it. Do you want something to drink? Milk? A cordial?'

Aimee accepts a cordial, and offers to help. 'No,' says the old lady, fluttering her hands at the idea. 'Sit down, sit down. We can't have our guest doing the work.'

Aimee takes a chair. The table is laid with a white cloth and two settings; Agatha adds a third. The kitchen is large and rather gloomy, but the gloom is fragrant with the smell of baking food. Tacked to the wall is a souvenir tea-towel, and a framed copy of *Desiderata*. 'Where do you think Kitten has gone?' Aimee asks, for there is nothing for her to say.

'I've no idea, darling. He wanders in and out as he pleases. Sometimes he's here, sometimes he's not: he gets very cross if I pry. You didn't bring your friend with you?'

'Oh, no, Curtis is busy.'

'Busy on a Sunday!' Agatha opens the oven and shuffles trays with a padded hand. 'Doesn't he ever give himself a rest?'

'No.'

'I couldn't bear to live like that, could you?'

Aimee shakes her head. 'No.'

'Kitten never seems to rest, either. He's always up to something.'

'Does Kitten work?' Aimee asks. The question comes

to her from nowhere and seems strangely impolite, but she is curious to know. He had been so evasive on the matter at her house two nights before. 'Does he have a job?'

Agatha is pouring frozen peas into a saucepan. She hesitates, glancing over her shoulder at her visitor. She takes a moment to compose her words. Then she says, 'Kitten helps me around the house. He helps take care of his grandfather. There's lots of heavy lifting, things I can't manage. He gives Mr Latch his baths, turns him over in his bed so he doesn't get sore. It's continuous work, looking after an invalid. I really think I admire Kitten for the things he does. At his age there's a hundred other things he'd prefer to be doing. But Kitten is very patient and good about it, he never complains. I couldn't manage without him. Mr Latch wouldn't care for a stranger looking after him, he wouldn't abide a professional nurse. So Kitten is indispensable, around here. I give him a little out of the housekeeping money from time to time. I give it to him on the sly, I don't tell Mr Latch, not that he could say or do much about it if he knew. But Kitten deserves it. He's a young man, he needs to get away from here sometimes, he should be out seeing the world, not stuck in here with a pair of decrepit fogies.'

As she speaks she continues to work: she has shaved slivers from the lump of meat and added them to a plateful of bread and baked vegetables. She cuts the food into small pieces. When it is done she says to

Aimee, 'Could you excuse me for a minute, dear? I'll go and give Mr Latch his dinner. Once that's finished we can eat in peace.'

She takes the plate and leaves the kitchen, and Aimee looks down at her hands. Now and then she turns to the back door, hoping to see Kitten come wheeling up the drive, dump his bike and walk inside, full of apology. Through this door she can see the back garden, the small tottering shed, the large cage where the ghastly naked bird is kept. Scattered through the garden beds, tiny spears of jonquil are poking through the earth. The fence is ringed with stringy oleander, the plant Kitten said was poisonous. From somewhere she hears a lawn being mowed, but there is no other sound. Though it is warm, the misty rain is falling, and Aimee thinks of winter.

Long minutes pass, and she gets up from her seat. The peas are boiling in their water, and she extinguishes the flame. She wanders about the room, skimming her fingertips over the surfaces. Finally she walks out into the hall. She hears the muffled voice of Agatha from behind the first closed door, coaxing the invalid to eat. The middle door has a posy of dried flowers dangling from its handle, the petals warped and brown. The third door stands ajar and she taps on it with her knuckles. The door drifts back from her touch, rocking on its hinges. She pushes it open and steps through: this is Kitten's room.

It is a small room and very light, for the curtains are

pulled and tied. The walls, pale green, were painted long ago; the carpet is beige and flattened. A single bed stands in the centre of the room and she's never seen a bed placed in such a way before, so far from the security of any wall. It is a neat little bed with a red quilt, a white pillow, a black cast-iron bedhead. Behind the door are a cupboard and a dresser and the only thing on the dresser is a large, ornamental urn. And this is all: there are no clothes on the floor, no pictures on the walls, no books on a shelf, no mirror for him to see himself. She wonders what Kitten spends his money on: on nothing, it seems, that might amuse him.

She shuts the door and hurries back to the kitchen wondering what she's doing, snooping around another person's private place.

Agatha returns a moment after Aimee takes her seat, carrying the plate, from which hardly any food has gone. 'Silly old fool's trying to starve himself to death,' she tells Aimee. 'Oh, thank you for looking after the peas, I forgot them. Kitten's not home yet? Well, we'll have to start without him. You don't mind, do you? I wouldn't want this meat to cool.'

She carves the meat carefully with her knotty hands, drains the peas, puts potatoes and pumpkin in decorative bowls. She forks food onto Aimee's plate and sets some aside for Kitten, leaving the least pleasing bits for herself. When it is done she sits opposite Aimee and says, 'Well, cheers. It's lovely to have a guest. I'm very cross at Kitten for leaving you like this. Boys can be thoughtless like that. I hope you don't mind, having to eat with an old lady. You'd probably go to your grandmother's for lunch now and then, though, don't you?'

'I used to, when I was little. My grandparents are dead now.'

'Oh, I'm sorry. Still, they're in a better place. Kitten's grandmother is dead, too. That's how I came to be living here. I was married to Mr Latch's brother, but he died in an accident, so I was alone. I've no children, you see. And then Kitten's grandmother Gloria died, and Mr Latch was here with Kitten, one a sick man and one just a boy, so I moved in, to look after them both. Oh, aren't I gruesome, talking about death at the table. When you're my age, you start to think about it sometimes.'

'I don't mind,' says Aimee, and breaks apart a piece of crusty bread. She is feeling more relaxed now, the meal is sweet and good, she's reminded of how it was to be a child, the focus of attention. The old woman is watching her with interest and admiration. 'What happened to Kitten's parents?' Aimee asks. 'Have they died, too?'

'Oh, goodness, no. The Reaper hasn't got his hands on everyone yet. No, Kitten's is a sad story – sadder, really, than if his parents had died. His father is Mr Latch's son. He was never married to Kitten's mother. I've never met her, but I've not a good word for her. She turned tail and left the boy when he was a toddler.

And the father – oh, he's hopeless. He's a hopeless man. He couldn't care for the child and didn't want to, I think. He couldn't go gallivanting with a little one in tow. So he brought the baby here, to his own mother's house, and asked her to care for the mite. I think it was the best thing the pair of them ever did, getting out of Kitten's life.'

'Sad for Kitten, though,' Aimee suggests. 'It's not nice, not to be wanted.'

'Wretched, is what it was. Because of course Mr Latch didn't want to take the child in, he'd never liked his own son, let alone the son of the son. Mr Latch grew up in another time, in the Depression, when everyone had to fight to exist. It made a lot of people very hard, very severe. He said the child was the responsibility of its parents, not him. Poor little Kitten, he was barely four and no one wanted him. Except Gloria, his grandmother, she wanted him. I think it was the only time she ever stood up to her husband's tyranny – she was a feeble woman, and he had walked all over her since the day she married him. What he said was law. But she stood up to him, then: I'd never seen her so determined. Someone had to care for the child, and she knew she was the only one left.'

Aimee presses potato and peas to her fork, dips it in the puddle of gravy. She thinks of Curtis: what would Curtis say to an unwanted child at the door?

'So Gloria took him in,' Agatha continues, 'and she adored the child, she spoiled him terribly, which of course Mr Latch thought was dreadful. It drove him mad, to see the boy ruined, and he'd bully the poor creature, worse even than how he'd bullied his own son. He'd never let the child leave the yard, or go to birthday parties, or buy him pretty clothes or nice things to eat or the toys his school fellows had. He'd terrorise him if he did badly at school, or accidentally broke a thing. He'd only let the child bathe in left-over bath water. He never had a good thing to say about anything the child did: he treated Kitten like a dog, really, how a man who hates animals might treat a dog. He'd say, This was how I was reared, and it didn't harm me. And it's true, Mr Latch was reared in hard times, but there's never been a time when brutality has been acceptable, has there? But Gloria always did her best to protect Kitten, to make his life happy. She'd sneak him small presents and chocolates, and let him watch television when the old fool wasn't around. And then the very worst thing happened: Gloria died. It stunned us all, she didn't seem the sort to just up and die. Kitten was eight. He'd been living here for about five years. Gloria was the only loving person he'd ever known. So he was alone again, but alone with his grandfather, and Mr Latch by this stage was a cripple, his legs were stiff as planks. More gravy?'

'Oh yes, please. It's delicious, Agatha, much nicer than the sandwich I'd have at home.'

'Then you should come every Sunday, we always have a roast. Gloria cooked one for her husband every

Sunday of her married life. When I arrived, I just continued the tradition.'

'So you came here after Gloria died, to look after the
two of them?'

'That's right. I'd known Mr Latch for years, I knew
his crotchety ways. And of course the boy needed
someone to care for him. I thought it would be fun,
finally having a child to look after. Mind you, I was
growing older myself by then. I was fifty. A fifty-year-
old woman, responsible for a child for the first time in
her life! I don't know what I was thinking. But he was
lovely, Kitten. He was the prettiest little thing you've
ever seen. He was never any trouble. Do you want to
see some photos? I'll show you some photos.'

She gets up from the table and hurries from the
room, returns with a slim album. She props the book
on the table and turns the pages, showing Aimee
photos of a boy standing in the garden, astride a black
pony, sitting at the front of his class. He bears a scratch
on his cheek in one, from coming too close to a cat.
Agatha's face is full of fondness as she turns the pages
over, pointing him out in group shots although he is
always easy to spot, his white hair marks him out.

'When he was little he'd come out of his room in the
morning in his pyjamas, all sleepy and hardly awake,
and that hair of his would be tangled and knotted up
at the back, a bird's nest, you could see every move
he'd made in the night . . .'

She turns the pages, points out her husband, and

Gloria, and a dim shot of Kitten's father. Aimee feels the story come alive as she looks at them, the players in the drama. At the final page Agatha closes the album, and strokes its cover. 'One day,' she says, 'his father turned up out of the blue. I remember I thought he'd come to take Kitten away. If he'd tried to take that child, oh, how I would have fought him. Kitten was mine by then, you see, mine, my responsibility. He was small and needed care then, not strong like he is now, so I knew I would need to do the fighting for him. I was ready to do so – part of me longed to do so. But the father seemed to find the child boring, and he only stayed an hour or so before pelting off in his fast car. I was glad to see the end of him, but Kitten stood in the street for a long time afterwards, as if he thought the man might remember him, and come back. It made me feel . . . awfully sad.'

Aimee's plate is empty now, her glass is drained. Agatha lifts her head and smiles. 'He's really helped me as much as I've ever helped him,' she says. 'I came here to look after him, but he gave me a reason to live.'

'That's nice,' Aimee whispers. 'That's so nice.'

She does not stay much longer after the meal, and she goes home without seeing Kitten. It is mid-afternoon and Curtis is watching football on television. Ptolemy is curled on his lap and she picks the animal up and drops it on the floor and takes its place on his knees, laying her head on his shoulder.

'How was lunch?' he asks. He does not shift his eyes from the screen.

'Good. I like it there. It's so old-fashioned. It's like another world.'

'Old-fashioned isn't another world, it's a dead world.'

'But it's lovely, Curt. You should come and have a look. There's food, and it's warm . . . Do you want to? Come to visit, I mean. I could ask Kitten –'

'No, I don't want to, Aimee. Leave me out of this cuteness.'

She sits up on his knees, and he is forced to look around her. 'It would probably do you good,' she says.

'I doubt it.'

'Well it does me good, so I wish you wouldn't make fun.'

Curtis sighs. 'I am not making fun,' he promises. 'How is your friend?'

'Kitten? He wasn't there. You should hear the story of his life, Curt, it is so sad –'

'Everyone's life is sad,' says Curtis.

'That's not true. My life hasn't been sad, and neither has yours. You're not sad now, are you? You're happy, aren't you? Living here, with me, doesn't that make you happy?'

'Yeah, yeah, you know I am, I was joking.'

She looks at him. 'We've always had people to love us,' she says. 'But Kitten's mother abandoned him, and his father didn't want him.'

'I'm not surprised,' quips Curtis, and laughs, but he does not get the reaction he expects, for Aimee doesn't laugh too. She springs from his lap and yells at him.

'God, Curtis!' she yells. 'I can't even have a conversation with you, can I? You sit there so bloody smug and pleased with yourself, you're just like that stupid cat! You're really heartless, aren't you? Heartless. I hate the way you are. You don't care a thing for other people. You probably don't even care for me. All you care about is your idiot computers and your equally idiot self!'

'Aimee –' he says, but she is gone, flinging herself from the room in a rage. He hears her go out the back door, letting the screen bounce noisily behind her. He thinks he should probably follow her, but grips the arms of his chair. Her behaviour is ridiculous and childish and he will not let himself appear the guilty party. Stubbornly he returns his gaze to the television screen, but the players scuttle on the edge of his concentration.

They have been going out with each other for three years, since meeting at an evening class that taught typing – she was learning it to boost her chances of getting a job, he because he was painfully slow on the keyboard and a frustration to himself. She was a quiet, pretty girl when she caught his attention, and she has remained much the same: he does not think he could ever like any girl who was raucous and heavy-handed. His family likes her, and he likes hers well enough. She is acceptable to his friends and colleagues at dinners and social gatherings, where she excels at idle chatter and never drinks enough to become offensive and a bore. He does not think he's ever been wildly in love with her, but he can't imagine being wildly in love with anyone. She, on the other hand, is devoted to him, and this charms him. She has a sense of humour that pleases him, for it is neither too sharp nor too evident, and she is easy to keep amused. She is docile and tidy and cautious with her money. She is also five years younger than himself, and if he has never found her an intellectual challenge, this is no concern to him, he thinks he must prefer it that way. He likes her for her cooking, for her company, because she is flattering when she walks alongside him. He is, more than anything, accustomed to having her around. He has never thought deeply on the state of their relationship, for there has never been a need: Aimee is as dependable as the seasons. At least, until lately, she has been. Since moving into this house she has behaved erratically, irrationally, she snipes about things that have never bothered her before. The thought that she finds his work idiotic affronts and hurts him. He had thought the upheaval of shifting out of home must be wearing on her – his father has taught him that women are fragile and prone to unusual moods and troubles – but now it occurs to him that she only behaves in this way, in this ridiculous and childish and ultimately embarrassing manner, whenever she has been visiting the house next door. Curtis sits in his chair and the cat comes to stand before him, staring at him with yellow eyes. He reaches down, to pat its head. She is out in the rain: well, let her stay there.

Outside, Aimee wanders through the garden. The rain ghosts down on her fair hair. She is sobbing miserably, and wringing her hands. She feels an intense anger at Curtis yet she is distraught and confused. He has done nothing wrong, but the desire to wound him had been so strong, it had been an absolute pleasure to scream her words at him, to cut him as deeply as she could. Inside she feels she is breaking into pieces. Her limbs seem heavy and dull, as if she's imprisoned in something that does not live. She rests her head against a tree trunk and weeps. She wants to go home, she wants a new life, she wants to die. When Kitten touches her shoulder she feels such a flood of relief that she thinks she truly might die, and spins around into his arms.

'Kitten,' she sobs, 'where have you been, where have you been?'

'Aimee,' he says, 'what has happened to you?'

She presses her face against his chest, smelling the smoky scent of him, feeling the curve of his bones. He has his hands on her shoulders and she wants him to hug her, squeeze her, take her away from here. 'That bloody Curtis,' she burbles. 'I hate him, sometimes I just want to kill him –'

Kitten chuckles, and she peers up at him through wet eyes. 'Poor Curtis,' he says. 'Didn't he take you out yesterday? Didn't you have a good day together?'

'Oh, yes,' she says. She clings to Kitten's shirt with fists. 'We went to the beach. It wasn't raining there.'

'You played in the water?'

'Oh, yes –'

'And didn't you have a nice time with him?'

'Yes,' she says, 'but today he's being an arsehole and I hate him.'

Kitten smiles. The twins whisper to him with scratching, gnashing voices. He carefully unclenches her fingers from his clothes. 'Go back inside, Aimee,' he tells her. 'Don't mind what Curtis says about me. Everything will be all right.'

He leans down and kisses her, lightly and on the cheek. She knows it is only a simple kiss to comfort her but, as she shambles back to the house, the place where he kissed her gently burns.

He dances into Paul's room, exultant. The twins are squealing, demanding to be heard. He disregards them, for they only wish to tell him things he already knows. Paul Latch is a man who's always hated the flamboyant sound of laughter, and this makes Kitten laugh all the more. He slumps against the bedstead and hangs there, giggling, his arms dangling over the wooden frame.

'Paul!' he chirps. 'You would not believe the fun I've been having. Yes, fun. Don't like that word, do you? Fun! Fun!'

His grandfather hisses at him and Kitten quietens, biting his lip. His hearing is sharp, and so is his sense of smell, and he detects the scent of roast vegetables lingering in the room. There are other smells: wood polish, musty clothes and, below this, the reek of the old man's decline. This Kitten can detect as easily as any animal. Soon the man will die: death is already in the room. The affliction is readying itself to sink deeply into the torso, freezing the organs one by one. Kitten pinches his lip with his teeth, and keeps the knowledge to himself.

'I've become friendly with the people next door,' he says. 'You remember: the young lady, the young man. Does that annoy you? I'm sorry if it does. The young man, he's becoming troubled by the thing, too. Not her, though: she likes me. The young man is a fool. An arrogant and self-absorbed fool. And she's beginning to see that this is so. Every day the distance between them yawns wider, and they can scarcely understand how, or why. It is, I must say, very diverting.'

He sighs contentedly, and his blue gaze drifts the length of Paul's body. He tweaks the toes of the old man's left foot.

'You'll say I'm being selfish,' he says, 'and I've a horrible feeling I should agree with you. I've been neglecting you, haven't I? I'm all caught up in amusing myself, and you've been lying here neglected. Derelict of me. I apologise. But don't worry, Paul: my thoughts are never far from you. I haven't forgotten you – I can't forget you, can I? I'll never leave you to suffer alone. And now I think it's curtain time.'

'Bastard, bastard, bastard,' seethes Paul Latch. His

grandson pays him not one scrap of attention. He crosses the room and draws back the curtains and the view of the garden opens into the room. Paul Latch dashes his head from side to side, his rage momentarily defying the paralysis in his neck. Kitten lifts his eyebrows, disconcerted by the action, and even the twins go still, jabbing their fangs into the rims of their mouths.

'Deviant,' gags his grandfather. 'You fucking fucking deviant –'

'Swearing is ugly in one so close to the worms,' Kitten replies darkly.

'You'll die!' splutters the invalid. He is coughing and choking, shooting spittle into the air. 'You'll die, you die, you die!'

Kitten smirks. 'You have always been an ungracious man, Paul,' he says. 'I admire your determination to remain so until the end.'

Paul is exhausted from struggling inside a frame that will not move: he hauls in air and his eyes skitter in their sockets. Kitten watches him for a long and wary minute; finally he says, 'Paul, calm yourself. You'll live a while longer. Shall I get you a glass of water?'

Paul hears him above his hoarse panting, he is never able to shut the devil's words from his ears. He wants the water but will not take it, he'll take nothing from the fiend, won't leave himself open to tricks and mockery. Kitten waits for a reply but gets none, so he turns back to the window. They are both unsettled now and even the twins are upset, whining like dogs in Kitten's ears. Kitten taps the windowsill and waits for them to quieten.

'Look at this rain,' he murmurs. 'Isn't it a curious rain? It's hardly here at all, and yet here it is. I imagine the swamp is slowly filling up with it. Oh, see there, the young man's cat is walking up our drive. On its way to stalk our Cocky, I suppose.'

Paul groans, and Kitten smiles, victorious. The last word must always be his.

ALL OVER THE world, people are watched. Curtis, up from his seat to let his complaining cat out the door, watches through a window as Kitten bends to kiss his – Curtis's – girlfriend. No one lives in a house or walks in the streets without being seen. People are watched by those who wish to do them harm, but more often they are watched by those they have harmed. Those who hurt others always have eyes upon them: wickedness is watched. Sometimes, when there is evil enough, that evil comes to life, and sets up home with you.

The week hauls itself along. On the television the weatherman points out the vast cloudy swirl that has brought all this peculiar and bothersome rain. On lines in the neighbourhood, articles of clothing hang lank and saturated. It is not cold but it feels as though it should be, and smoke comes out of chimneys. In schoolyards children stomp in gathering puddles and lick the rain from their faces. The weather dampens letters in mailboxes and depresses dogs locked outside in yards.

Each day Aimee drags herself off to work again. The tram tracks glisten with wetness, causing cars to veer.

She finds her job tedious, repetitive, and stupid. They treat her as a lowly thing here, someone to be ordered about. Around her they hush their voices, deeming their conversations not suitable for her hearing. No one asks her opinion: she is told what to do and is expected to do only it and nothing more. Her hands grow cold on the keyboard. She begins to think that she was born for something better than typing other people's mail.

At night she lies beside Curtis and hears the droplets fall from the guttering. Sometimes she gets out of bed for a glass of milk or some toast and she sees, then, light, yellowing the garden beyond Kitten's bedroom. She wishes she could visit him but she has been reared knowing not to impose herself, knowing he'll show himself when he wishes to be seen.

On Friday morning she hands in her resignation. 'I couldn't stand it any more,' she explains to Curtis.

Curtis is astounded, and furious. 'What the hell do you think you're doing?' he gags. 'What do you think you're going to do?'

'I don't like it there, Curt. Do you want me to stay in a place I hate?'

'Aimee, we've got rent to pay! I'm trying to set up my own business! Do you think we can do that on one income?'

'I'll get another job,' she says, reluctantly.

'How? How will you get another job? There are no jobs to be had!'

'I don't want to be a secretary,' she mumbles. 'I hate being that. That's only important to other people. I want to be something that's important to me.'

'Like what?' he barks. 'What can you do? You don't know how to do anything else!'

'Maybe I'll go to university –'

'I can't afford to keep you while you sit around at some bloody school! God, Aimee, if I'd known you were going to do this, I'd never have come here in the first place!'

'Oh, you don't want to live with me?'

'We had an agreement, Aimee. You know this can't work if you're hanging around doing nothing like that freak next door!'

'What agreement?' she yells, furious now herself. 'If there was an agreement, I was never told about it! I'm pleased to know you wanted to live with me for my pay cheques, Curtis!'

'That's not what I meant, and you know it –'

'I'll do whatever I feel like doing!' she screeches. 'Maybe I'll dig ditches by the road! Maybe I'll have a stall at a market and read tarot cards! Maybe I'll cook drugs in the garage! Maybe, for the first time in my life, I'll do something I want to do! What's so bad, Curtis, about doing something for the love of it?'

He backs off in the face of her anger. He's never had a shouting argument with her before, and now she looks quite dangerously wild. 'Listen,' he says. 'Why don't we have a cup of tea and talk about this calmly?

I assume they've given you the chance to change your mind, haven't they?'

Aimee stares at him; her shoulders slump, and she sighs. 'You're a brick wall, aren't you,' she mutters. 'You're just a bloody stupid brick bloody wall.'

All evening she is sullen with him, and all morning of the following day. She refuses to talk about the problem. When he mentions it, she looks at him with sad disgust. After lunch on Saturday, he goes and knocks on Kitten's door. Curtis is the type of person who feels he has the right to impress his opinion.

The door is opened by Agatha. 'Hello,' she says. 'You're from next door, aren't you? It's a pleasure to meet you.'

'Can I speak to Kitten?' The name sticks in his craw.

Agatha calls, 'Kitten!' and disappears into the house. Curtis waits, his fists pushed grimly in his pockets, until Kitten steps from behind the door. He gives his visitor a cool smile. 'Curtis,' he says. 'What a surprise. What may I do for you? Have you come to borrow a cup of sugar, perhaps?'

'I want to talk to you,' says Curtis, severely.

'Oh? Would you care to come inside, out of the rain?'

'No.' Curtis wants Aimee to see this if she is looking out the window. 'Just here will do.'

'As you wish.' Kitten leans against the door. He does not seem intimidated: he lights a cigarette, and offers Curtis the open pack. Curtis impatiently refuses.

'Aimee and I have been living next door to you for two weeks,' he begins. 'I don't know about you, but it seems a hell of a lot longer to me. I don't like the way Aimee's been behaving since we arrived. She argues with me; now she's quitting her job. Wants to do something for the love of it: where do you think she got that idea? You're filling her head with horse shit. Every time she sees you she starts acting weird with me. I don't like it, and I'm sick of it. I want you to stay away from her. I don't want you asking her into your house. I don't want you coming into our house, either. If she invites you, you'll refuse.'

Kitten blinks at him. 'Hmm,' he says.

'You know nothing about Aimee,' Curtis says. 'I've known her for three years. I know you don't think much of me, I know you don't respect the things I do, and that's fine, I couldn't care less. But when you start messing about with my life you're going too far. I love Aimee. One day I'm going to marry her. We'll have a few kids, we'll live in a nice house. I'll be making a lot of money by then. I can give her whatever she wants, then. In the meantime, things are different. She knows that. She knows I care for her, even if sometimes I'm too busy to show it. We've got things sorted between us, things you wouldn't understand.'

Kitten draws on his cigarette and appears to consider this. Inside his head the twins are screaming at him to move. They writhe their slick naked bodies, they crash their razor teeth. They're urging Kitten to pinch Curtis in half. Kitten thinks carefully around them: they are primitive, they lack finesse. In the silence, sweat breaks out on Curtis's brow. He draws a fist from his pocket and prods Kitten sharply in the chest.

'This is my life,' he says. 'It's got nothing to do with you. If you start meddling with your sticky fucking fingers, I'll break every single one of them off your hands. Do you understand?'

'Yes,' says Kitten Latch, 'I suppose I do.'

'Good. I'm going back home now, and it's the last time I want to see you anywhere near me or anything that is mine.'

'As you say, then.'

His composure is infuriating to Curtis: it makes him stagger back. 'I saw you kiss her,' he splutters. 'I'm not the jealous type: I know you did it because she was upset. But that's as close as you get, understand? Never again. Never again, or you'll pay.'

He wheels on his feet and stomps away, and Kitten watches him go. Not thoroughly satisfied, Curtis marches down the driveway and along the footpath without looking back. Kitten stays by the door until his cigarette is finished. He sends the butt spinning into the garden. The noise of the outraged twins is hurting his head.

He goes to Paul's room, and sits on the bed. The old man is dozing, but wakens when he feels the weight. He squints uneasily at his grandson. Kitten sits with his hands on his knees, looking over his shoulder at the old man.

'I have the young man running scared now, Grandfather,' he says softly. 'He is afraid of me. He came here to make me fear him, but he is the one who is afraid.'

'You're afraid,' mutters the invalid. Kitten's face remains expressionless, and the old man cackles tauntingly. 'Afraid, afraid, you're afraid.'

Kitten stares at him for a moment. Then he leans across the bed so he is very close to the withered head on the pillows. 'If you could talk like you could when I was a child,' he says, 'if you could talk above a hopeless whisper, if you could thunder like you did when you were king of your tiny castle and you roared your tyrannical orders to a frail woman and a helpless child and they obeyed or risked your violence, a slap to the face, a blow to the chin – well, then you could tell that young man what he is up against. Unfortunately, as you're now so pathetically disabled, he must discover that for himself.'

Ptolemy lies on his side in the middle of the road. It is Sunday morning. The rain has been falling upon him and his grey coat has soaked black. The people walking home from Mass wince at the sight of him, and turn their eyes away. Cars, when they reach him, swerve to one side. No one wants him flatter than he is.

Curtis crouches in the gutter, and Aimee stands

beside him. 'Oh, Curtis,' she says, 'I'm sorry. I know how much you loved him.'

The cat's eyes are bulging, testimony to its last moment of terrible fright. Curtis hangs his head and the rain falls warm on the back of his neck.

'What will we do? We can't just leave him there . . .'

'I'll bury him in the garden.'

Aimee draws a breath. Then she tells him, 'We don't have a spade.'

Curtis says nothing. He puts a hand to his face.

'I'll borrow one from next door, shall I?'

'Yes,' he says, and his voice catches in his throat. 'That would be appropriate.'

She runs over to Kitten's house, dashes up the drive to the back door. Kitten is in the kitchen, playing cards at the table. When he's told she needs a spade because Ptolemy is dead, he says, 'Oh, I'm sorry, that's awful, I'm sorry.'

He makes her wait in the shelter of the kitchen while he goes to the shed and brings out a large spade, and she runs with it back to where Curtis crouches in despair. She says, 'Here, I'll help you.'

'No,' he says, savagely. 'I'll do it myself. You go inside.'

She looks down at him but he does not lift his head or stand up, so after a moment she turns and goes into the house. From the laundry window she watches him carry the carcass to the elm tree, balancing the weight with care. He lowers the cat to the ground and slips it from the spade, and then he digs the hole. The work is laborious, for the ground is riddled with tree roots, but he is strong and he uses his strength. Nonetheless it takes a long time, and in the rain he gets very wet. When the hole is deep enough he goes to the garage and brings out a box and an old cloth, which he wraps around the cat. He lays the animal in the box and the box in the hole, and begins to fill it in. Aimee goes to the front garden and cuts some flowers and she brings them out to Curtis, together with his raincoat. She lays the coat across his shoulders and the flowers on the grave, then puts an arm around his waist.

'He was a good cat,' she says. 'He had a good life.'

'You know who's responsible for this, don't you?'

For an instant she thinks he means her, for it was she who had let the creature out that night after it yowled and scrabbled at the door: she steps backwards, ready with guilty protests. But Curtis looks across at Kitten's ramshackle fence and she says, 'Oh, Curtis, no.'

'He could do it. He'd do it.'

'Curt, don't be silly, it's been run over by a car –'

Curtis snaps his head round to glare at her. 'Did you see it happen?' he asks. 'Did you see a car come up and did you see him go under the wheels?'

'No, but –'

'Then you don't know anything about it.'

'Curtis, this is silly, you can't blame Kitten!'

He jerks a lip and swings away, heading back to the house; she knows she is not invited to follow. He'll hide himself in his study and possibly cry, though she's never seen him cry. She takes the spade and washes it under a tap, then hefts it and goes around to the house next door.

Kitten is still playing cards at the kitchen table. It is an elaborate game, one she's never seen before. It needs two packs, one dealt out straight and in order, the other forming a curling spiral. 'You needn't have returned it today,' he tells her. 'It can wait.'

'I don't think Curtis wants me around,' she explains.

'He doesn't want you here, either.'

'Did he say that to you?'

'It makes me wonder what place you have left to go. Can I make you a cup of tea?'

She accepts gratefully, and sits opposite his seat at the table. She examines the layout of the cards. 'What's this game you're playing?' she asks.

'Oh – it's complicated –'

'Too complicated for me, you mean.'

Kitten turns and looks at her. 'Not at all,' he says. 'What makes you say that?'

Aimee hesitates, and sighs. 'Habit,' she says.

He settles the kettle on the stove and returns to sit before her. 'It's a game to pass the time,' he says. 'I'll teach it to you one day.'

'Teach me now.'

He shakes his white head. 'No,' he says, 'we've plenty of time.'

She smiles. She has a sense of tranquillity when she is around Kitten: she thinks she could tell him anything and he would not laugh at her, she could ask anything of him and he'd do it if he could. 'Where's Agatha?' she asks. 'I like her.'

'Of course,' he says. 'Agatha is an angel.'

'She looks after you.'

'She watches over me, that is true.'

'Where has she gone, then? Back to heaven?'

'There's no heaven,' says Kitten. 'I believe she's gone to visit her sister.'

Aimee smiles again, girlishly. It makes Kitten blush faintly, unwillingly, and look down at his cards. The twins are very still.

'The object of this game,' he says, 'is for the Jack to complete his task of going through the world, meeting friends and enemies. These cards in line keep the score; the cards in a circle are the players in the world.'

'How does the Jack know who are friends, and who are enemies?'

'The enemies are dealt out for him; the friends are attracted to him. The enemies are many, the friends are rather rare.'

'How do his friends help him?'

The kettle is boiling and Kitten gets up to make the tea. He rinses the pot and spoons in the leaves. 'They give him protection,' he explains. 'Sometimes, they sacrifice themselves.'

'It's like chess, then?'

'In chess,' he says, 'the King is assured of the loyalty of the other pieces.'

'And your Jack isn't?'

'The Jack must watch everyone. Sometimes, his friends will turn against him. They're not always to be trusted.'

'You made this up by yourself? It's amazing.'

'I didn't make it up. It's an ancient game. So old it has no name. Before it was played with cards, I think it was played with stones.'

'Old,' Aimee agrees. Kitten smiles, and props his elbows on the kitchen bench.

'The enemies have strength,' he says. 'The lowest cards are the weakest, the Aces are the strongest. The friends, too, have strength. If the Jack is lucky he will find his matching Ace, which is his strongest friend. This makes life easier for him.'

'It's a bit bad for the poor Jack, isn't it? So many enemies, so few true friends.'

'Oh, don't feel sorry for him. You see, in this game, the Jack always wins. It's pre-ordained. His task is finished before it's begun. Even the strongest enemy is never strong enough. We have cakes,' he says. 'May I offer you some?'

She grins at the table-top. She likes the way he talks, so proper and old-fashioned. He brings to her a plate of small cakes dabbed with icing and fresh cream, and he tells her, 'You must eat them. Agatha made them for you.'

The smell of them is glorious; the taste of them is superb. She crams one and then another into her mouth, washing them down with gulps of tea. 'I love this house,' she mumbles, through a mouthful of crumbs. 'I just love being here.'

'It is a pity Curtis won't let you visit as you please.'

'Curtis is going crazy,' she tells him. 'He thinks you killed his cat.'

Kitten flicks up an eyebrow. 'Does he indeed? How did I manage that?'

'Oh, I don't know –'

'Perhaps I took it into my shed,' suggests Kitten, 'and flattened it out with a hammer?'

'Don't say that –'

'Why not? Don't you think I could do it?'

Aimee stops licking icing off her fingertips: she gazes at Kitten and says, 'Please tell me you didn't do that.'

'I didn't,' he sighs. He drums his nails on the specked laminex and adds, 'It bothers me that you doubt me.'

'I don't doubt you,' she hastens, regretting she's mentioned the matter. 'I can't imagine you ever harming a thing.'

'We all do harm aplenty,' he says shortly. 'It cannot always be helped. On occasion it is necessary. That is the nature of things.'

She wipes cake flecks from her chin. Kitten has turned his eyes away. Aimee's gaze drifts about the room and returns to the cards. 'Has your Jack got many friends?' she asks.

'Look,' he answers, 'the sun is shining. The rain has stopped.'

She twists in her chair to see the sky. 'Come with me,' says Kitten. 'I want to show you something.'

She follows him out into the wet garden, stepping in his footprints. He is wearing the kind of clothes he always wears, clothing such as Curtis never wears, for they suggest a lackadaisical approach. Long shirt, loose trousers, a vest that flicks the air behind him. The boots he wears are always black. The cockatoo's cage is dripping and the bird is hidden from sight. The oleander is bowed with the weight of the water. He goes to the shed and unbolts the door and waits for her to step past him, inside.

'Wow,' she says.

The shed is filled with things she's never seen before, but she recognises them as tools. Benches line two walls and there's a sink set into the third, and on the floor are boards dusted with papery shavings. On every surface and hung from nails around the walls are tools of every sort imaginable, hacksaws, fretsaws, chisels, and shears; there are lanterns, picks, axes and great clawed hoes. There are racks of curving sickles and long-bladed scythes, there's an anvil on the floor for keeping open the door. All of them are old tools, nothing is plastic or new. They are heavy tools from another time, when wood and iron were the materials used, and things were held together with rivets, nails, and chains. Most of the tools have been lovingly restored: there are scalpels and scourers, wire wheels and braces all around the room. Along one bench are scattered plough blades brown with rust and age, on the other lies a bandy bushman's saw with worn handles at each end of the blade.

'Wow,' she says, again. 'So this is what you do.'

There is a single tall chair that Kitten dusts and draws out for her; he leans beside her, propping himself in the angle where the benches meet. The smell of linseed is strong in the air: the window is open but it is clogged with privet and curls of jasmine. Aimee lifts an ancient spindle and it spins and spins in her hands. 'That's a drill,' he explains. 'You see, the turning weight drives the drill bit in.'

She senses how proud he is of these things, and also the honour it is to be invited in. 'Why these?' she asks, and her voice is a reverential whisper. 'What is it you like about these?'

'Respect,' he says. 'The people who made these tools knew you needed iron and steel. They knew nature was something to be reckoned with. They knew you need to touch the world with the things you take from it. You can't do that with plastic and computers.'

The reference to Curtis reaches a hollow place in her heart and echoes around there until it grows dull and disappears. She runs a finger along the prickles of a rasp, feeling her flesh scratched up. There are tubs of grease and brushes in pots of black water, and a pretty saucer thieved from the kitchen which now holds screws and washers and tiny, tightly coiled springs. 'So this is what you do with your money,' she muses.

'Agatha told me she gives you money and I wondered what you spend it on. These things are beautiful.'

Beautiful, and also somehow dangerous, and she likes that about them. Each item he's chosen has a blade, a point, a robust weight, a set of biting teeth. The room, the smell, the waving of the jasmine, these things seem to hypnotise her. She says, 'Agatha told me all about you.'

'All about me? What did she say?'

'I saw things about you, too. I saw photographs. I even looked inside your room. That urn on your dresser – is that the ashes of your grandmother?'

Kitten shakes his head and smiles. 'Do you think I am morbid?' he asks. 'What would I want them for? That's where I keep my spare change. Tell me, what did Agatha say?'

'She told me the things that have happened in your life. About your parents. How you have been alone.'

'Oh,' he says, 'that. That is of no interest whatsoever. Did she tell you what is going to happen?'

'Going to happen?' Aimee looks across at him, frowning. 'How does anyone know what's going to happen?'

'Curtis knows. He's going to marry you and buy a big house and father a horde of children.'

'You say those words with such awful . . . contempt.'

'I cannot believe it will make you happy.'

'It's just something we've always talked about.'

'You do not even love him. You tell yourself you do,

but you do not. You have found someone you think you can endure, and you are trying to convince yourself that is love. He is less than ordinary. There is nothing worthy in him. For that, you are living on your knees.'

'There is nothing special or worthy about me either, Kitten –'

'Don't say that!' he snaps. He startles her with his vehemence, and himself. This was always meant to be a game, a simple exercise, and Aimee was only cast to be a pawn. What he has begun to feel for her should shame a devil, and he is ashamed, but he is not repentant. More deliberately he says, 'Maybe your family thinks little of you: merely a daughter, someone to wear ribbons and bows, they've never expected anything remarkable from you. Maybe Curtis thinks you're just a girl, like all those ever born. But you insult me, to number me amongst people such as they. I don't think of you like that. You are the first person I've ever brought here, do you know?'

She smiles bashfully, and he hurries on.

'Think of this, Aimee: if, tomorrow, everyone was given the chance to abandon the life they live and begin, instead, a life utterly new, an uncertain life, a reckless life – which would you choose? Which would Curtis choose?'

'I – I think Curtis wouldn't change.'

'No. He is happy.'

Aimee sighs, and toys listlessly with the spindle. Kitten watches her, and shifts his footing.

'When my grandfather dies,' he says, 'Agatha and I are going to leave this place. Everything we had to do here will be done. We're going to close this house and move to the country. There is a place there, by a creek, surrounded by fields. It is a small house, very old, and well away from the town.'

'Is it the house you went to when you were a child, the time your forgot your pyjamas?'

'It would be ironic, wouldn't it? To return to that place. It wouldn't be frightening to me now. It would be like returning to the beginning. It is not that place. It is a new, different, wilder place. There is room for you there, Aimee.'

She jerks her head up. 'Kitten,' she says, 'you know I can't –'

'Why not?'

'That's just pretending, Kitten! That's just a silly idea, that's not real –'

'Isn't it? Why not? Change your life, Aimee. You are being given the chance. You know all this is what you prefer. When you look at me, you see destiny.'

She stares at him. His eyes are fog-blue, watching her steadily.

'You shouldn't say things like that,' she says.

'It's true, though.'

'No,' she says, and her voice quavers. 'You don't understand. You don't seem to live in the same world everyone else lives in, Kitten. Things aren't easy, like you think they are. Life isn't a game, you don't go changing it just because you can. Everything I'll ever get is starting to come to me, now – how can I turn around, and hand back the things I've finally got?'

'Aimee, what have you got?'

She feels panic, desperation. She knows if she refuses now, she is lost. 'Kitten,' she groans, 'who are you, why are you here, what are you doing? Are you here just to torment me, to make me see how sad I am? Is that your purpose?'

'You owe him,' says Kitten, 'nothing.'

'I can't,' she says, pleadingly, and tears start to come. 'I can't make choices, not like this –'

'There is no choice. Look to your heart: what does it tell you?'

She looks, instead, into his eyes. 'It tells me nothing,' she whispers. 'My heart is a useless heart.'

'Aimee,' he says, and holds out a hand. She steps from the chair and into his arms. He draws her close, envelops her as if with wings. He bows his head and kisses her and she cries against his face. She knows she is only safe here, at this moment, pressed tightly against his body, she wants to tear him open and step inside him, where she'll be safer still. She does not resist him or the kisses over her face and when he tilts her chin up she lets him, exposing the flesh of her throat. He kisses her there and then bites her, so she feels a handsome pain. It is a pressure that starts softly and grows until she almost cries out, and suddenly it is gone. When she goes home that day she will wear the

72

marks of the devil, the clinging smell of oil, the bruising on her neck.

He holds her tightly, like something he means to keep. 'There's plenty of time,' he tells her, though he knows this will never be true.

He takes her hand and leads her out of the garden shed and she stumbles after him in a daze. The fresh air revives her, blows the roaring from her ears. She looks up at him, not knowing what to say. She would believe it had been a hallucination but for the faint throbbing of the flesh at her throat. She sees herself standing dumb there and collects herself, and gazes around.

'Your bird,' she says, 'why does it have no feathers?'

'It worries,' replies Kitten. 'They will grow back, it won't last forever. Are you going to work tomorrow?'

'Oh yes, I must.'

He nods. 'I'll see one or the other of you,' he says, 'before the week is done.'

He releases her hand, and she understands she is free to go.

In the kitchen he sweeps the cards aside. 'Kitten,' Agatha says, 'my Kitten –'

'Leave me,' he hisses. 'Leave me alone.'

'If it is not what she wants –'

'I know what she wants!'

'You may be making her more unhappy. Maybe it is a mistake, maybe she is meant to stay with the young man –'

'There is no mistake! I do not make mistakes! I am trying to do some good! You stupid old lunatic, may I never do any good?'

'Is it good, Kitten, to treat her as a prize that can be fought for and won? To treat her as a trophy, as the young man treats her – or as an object, as Paul treated his wife?'

'That is not what I am doing! How dare you compare me to that man! You understand nothing, Agatha, after all these years of living by my side you understand nothing about me! Look at me, what do you see? I am not like you, or like him, or like anyone, but she is like me!'

'How? How is she like you? Kitten, you must not try so hard –'

From the scattered cards he plucks the black Jack and its matching Ace, and brandishes them side by side.

'Look!' he snarls. 'This is what she is to me! One I never expected to find in the flesh. She looks at me, she listens to me. She waits for me, she watches for me. She is alone, as I am alone. I am important to her, and she must be of importance to me. The Ace card, Agatha! We have sought each other for centuries. Don't I deserve to have found her? Don't I deserve something, after all I've been through, after all I am condemned to?'

'You deserve nothing. It is wrong, to think you deserve anything.'

He drops the cards and they slide across the floor. For a long minute he stares at her, and Agatha stays silent and still. She loves him, but she also fears him. She has nothing that can compete with him, not her strength, not her age, nothing that she knows. An angel will always be felled by a devil. He turns from her, disgusted.

'Leave me,' he says. 'Leave me be. Do what you are supposed to do, and nothing more.'

He walks out and she, defeated, does not follow him. He takes his agitation to his grandfather's room and she is relieved he is gone.

At the sound of the door closing, Paul Latch opens his eyes. The stiffness has coiled around his ears, he can no longer move his head.

His grandson is in the room. He is pacing the floor and Paul may see him only in glimpses. Kitten says nothing: he stalks from wall to wall in silence, waiting for the chattering voices to die down. The twins have been stirred by the argument, they are angry, angry at him, they say he handles things badly, he shouldn't need to defend what he does, he does not deserve to be what he is, he certainly does not deserve the benefit of them. He digs his nails into the flesh of his temples, wishing he could drag out the demons and fling them writhing to the floor, and of course they hear this thought and make him sorry for it, they sneer and spit and slash at him, full of scorn and unafraid.

'Listen,' he begs them. 'Listen to me –'

Paul has no choice but to listen.

'Didn't this rain fall for a reason? Didn't I bring it with a purpose? Don't you think the swamp will be full? If you will only listen, I can explain . . .'

His voice is imploring: Paul has not heard the tone since his grandson was a child. Kitten moans and rubs his fists into his eyes: the twins make him feel as if his head must explode. 'I will not have you doubting me!' he yelps, suddenly enraged, and kicks the bedpost with force enough to make the great bed shudder.

Paul grunts in irritation: Kitten lifts his head and looks at him. After a moment he steps around the bed and stares down into his grandfather's eyes. The twins have quickly calmed themselves. In an instant they consider the situation. They have been losing patience with his interest in Aimee, it has been consuming too much of his time. The twins are driven, obsessive. Now they see how the diversion might be made useful, and they put to him the words he must say. He has no choice but to say it, for already they are tightening their grip.

'I am going to kill the young man next door,' is what Kitten tells his grandfather.

CURTIS LEAVES HIS work-place early. It is three o'clock on a clear and dry Monday afternoon when he strips off his suit and drops it to the floor and dresses himself instead in tracksuit pants and a t-shirt. His hands move very quickly, his steps are short and sharp. All night and all day his brain has been working, but he is not tired: indeed, he feels feverishly energised. He marches over to Kitten's house burning with anger and intensity.

Kitten is in the back garden, talking to the cockatoo. The bald head swivels when the creature spots Curtis crossing the yard, but Kitten does not look around. He lets Curtis yank his shoulder and spin him on his feet. His back hits the birdcage hard, the steel frame rattles, and the cockatoo begins to scream.

Curtis has his fists clenched at Kitten's collar. Kitten stares at him with faint surprise. 'Curtis,' he says, 'what may I do for you?'

Curtis shakes him fiercely, and the big cage shudders. 'You,' he growls. 'I'm going to kill you –'

Kitten glances at the house. 'Here?' he asks. 'Must it be done here?'

Curtis does not seem to hear. 'I asked you nicely to

stay away,' he says. 'I told you what would happen if you did not. What's enough for you, buddy? First my cat, then my girlfriend's coming home with marks all over her face!'

Kitten feels a mischievous desire to laugh, which he quells. 'I cannot say what happened to your cat,' he says. 'My guess is it was a stationwagon of some sort. As for Aimee, that is a different matter –'

Curtis howls, and swings a fist. It misses Kitten, and Curtis stands baffled as to how. Kitten, a step clear of his assailant now, dusts his collar and looks at the young man. The bird continues to screech, throwing itself awkwardly from one perch to another. Kitten judges that the time for joking is over.

'Curtis,' he says. 'I understand what you feel you must do. It shall not, however, be done here. My aunt is elderly, and easily upset. Were she to glance from the window and see you in any way harming me, she would without doubt call the police. That is not something I imagine you want or need. An assault charge would have a jarring effect on anyone's curriculum vitae, agreed?'

Curtis stands poised, listening. Kitten feels pain pulsing through his spine, the places he will bruise.

'I am not unreasonable,' he says, his voice steady, his clear eyes fixed on the young man. 'It is right, that you should have your revenge. Allow me a last indulgence, then: collect your bicycle, and we shall go somewhere more private.'

Curtis stares at him. The cocky lurches the length of the cage with its beak open, its chest heaving. As Curtis watches Kitten his vision seems to cloud, he feels vaguely sleepy, his fury starts to drain. He thinks he'd prefer to be resting, reclining away what remains of the day. He knows, at that moment, what is unusual about this white, willowy boy.

'Forget it,' he sighs. 'Let's just forget it.'

Kitten smiles, showing a glimmer of teeth. He shakes his head sadly. 'But it cannot be forgotten,' he says. 'It simply cannot.'

So, unwilling to do what he does even as he is doing it, Curtis returns to his house to get his bicycle. That is the thing, of course: it is impossible, to refuse Kitten Latch.

Side by side they glide through the streets. The tyres of their bicycles spray droplets from the surface of the road and hiss the pleasant sound of speed. In this neighbourhood, at this time of day, nothing moves or makes a sound: dogs don't bark, birds don't sing, the old people are closeted in their houses. To the swamp it is all downhill.

Kitten bursts into his grandfather's room. He is panting, his eyes are bright, his hair is damp and wild. His trousers are wet below the knees, soaked with the pungent water of the swamp. It is only an hour since he left the house.

'Paul!' he shouts. 'Pauly, Pauly, wake up!'

Paul's eyes flutter open. He wonders if, when the stiffening reaches his eyelids, they'll be frozen closed or torturously wide. His grandson is leaning close to his face and in the dimness Paul sees that the boy's flesh is damaged, marked and torn around the eyes.

'I did it,' Kitten says, grinning, breathless. 'I did what I promised I would do. I have killed the young man next door. Do you want to know where he is, now? He's sunk into the swamp, his legs imprisoned in the muck. It pulled him down like quicksand, pressing the air from him as he went. In the summer, when the mud hardens and the water steams away, there he'll be, for everyone to see!'

Paul Latch widens his eyes at his grandson. Air snorts noisily from his nose. Kitten pushes himself away from the bed and skirts the room. There is a chair in the corner, draped with a towel. He throws the towel off and sits down, crossing his long legs.

'Mind if I smoke?' he asks, and lights a cigarette. He bounces a foot, flustered and excited. Paul must strain his eyes in their sockets to glimpse a flash of blond hair, a wave of a smoke-twined hand.

'I'm not making sense, am I?' babbles Kitten. 'I'll tell it from the start. You know, of course, that the young man wished to harm me – you'd understand that, wouldn't you? But you could have told him better, couldn't you? You'd have told him not to waste his time. He thought I feared him. I said to him at one stage, How can you believe that I, Kitten Latch, might

80

be afraid of little you? He didn't answer me. By that time, he'd realised the immensity of his mistake.'

Kitten laughs, remembering. He draws on his cigarette and blows a cloud of smoke above the bed. 'But I'm rushing,' he says, reprimanding himself. 'Nothing will be clear unless I explain it properly. We went to the swamp because it is my place, would you not agree? There's no place made better, for someone such as me. It was quiet there, as usual, and very still, and all this rain had brought the swamp water high, higher than it's ever been. We dragged our bikes through the bushes and our feet were sinking into the mud, making a wonderful sound. The water in the swamp is pale brown, almost white. Drifting on its surface are pools of grey foam. The trees rising out of it are grey, the colour of the water. They are hung with clusters of dead leaves, feathers, and rubbish blown in from the street. You know it's curious, because all around the swamp is grass and earth and trees that are green and healthy, but the swamp is wan and grey, like something that doesn't breathe. Two herons were there, treading through the mud: when they saw us they paused and then took off into the air. The young man couldn't understand why I'd brought him there, he couldn't see that this place is mine. By now he'd lost the desire to hit me, to hurt me, he'd have been content, I know, to explain politely what he'd previously wished to beat into me. But, of course, this new reluctance was not going to save him. Look Kitten, says he to me, I want you to stay away from Aimee. Don't make me have to tell you again. And I replied, I'm sorry Curtis, but I cannot possibly agree to that. You have lost and I have won, and this battle was over before it was begun. You think there is no place for one such as I in this world, but I'm afraid you are wrong. This is my world, and you and your breed are a nasty, invasive sore upon it. In an infinite universe this is a singular green planet, but you would make it so cold and hard it must soon be crisp. You will not do so: you will not wrap it in wires until it chokes. You will not hold nature in contempt, as something not quite so wily as yourselves. Most important of all, you will not make this a world where all must think as you do, making those who do not agree with you feel isolated and unworthy. You will not bully the world in a direction which you alone believe is forward. You have made the world something to be used, as you are using the girl. It is your aim to make it a place not for living, but for existing. You are dangerous, because you lack forethought. You think you lead well, but your leadership is despotic and blind. Your confidence is brutal, your determination is monstrous. Your kind has done much damage, and you will continue vainly to do much more. But you for one, my friend, are not going to do any more. This is my world, and I serve it by extracting those who harm it and others. Your precious machines will be black and grow dusty in your long, long absence.'

Kitten pauses, and sits up in his chair to see his

grandfather's face. The old man has grown colourless, his chest heaves laboriously up and down. Kitten drops his cigarette butt on the carpet, and crushes it under his heel.

'By now nothing was moving. The whole world had emptied for my purpose. I took mercy on him for a moment: I did not want him leaving without understanding. My task, I explained, is ancient, and I have worked to fulfil it for thousands of years. My determination is, therefore, much greater than yours, and I would not advise you to fight or flee. You will feel no more pain than that which you have inflicted: if I were allowed my way, I should like it to be more. But, there it is. Sleep well, Curtis, and if we meet again, I hope we can be friends.'

Paul Latch is making small mewling noises, which Kitten ignores.

'The swamp was at his ankles: it was a simple thing to push him in more deeply. In fear and anger he swiped a claw at my face, catching me under the eye. I did not begrudge him this, for we all bear the scars of our existence and there's something fine in that, don't you agree? It is proof that we have fought the battle well. The swamp was overly obliging and it held him fast, making him fall. He thrashed in the mud and water then, making a pathetic sight. I did not want to leave him there, where the birds and the animals might get at him, so I found a decent branch and I used it to prod him more securely in, towards the centre of the swamp. He was wet and heavy and weakening by now, he'd breathed in mud and it had got into his clothes, his legs were leaden, his mind was frail, it was really such a simple thing. Do you know how a person drowns, Paul? It's different in salt water than it is in fresh. Salt water sucks water from the circulation and into the lungs – fresh water goes from the lungs into the circulation. Curtis's blood will be mud. The gas in his flesh should, by rights, make him surface before long, but you and I know that will not happen. Ah, no, that's not going to happen.'

Paul's mewling has gone to gasping and, now, to strangled cries. Kitten feels the quickening of the old man's heart, hears its erratic jerks. He gets from his chair and leans close to the bed. The man's face is a yellow skull, the eyes are staring wide.

'He surprised me, though. When I thought he was finished he suddenly reached up an arm, an arm dripping with slop and slime. His head was under the water, he could not see or know what he was doing. By chance his hand gripped a low tree branch, and fastened to it for grim life. Alas, the moment he put weight upon it, that old tree branch splintered and broke. I guess that is what happens, when you deny nature: nature, in turn, denies you.'

Rigid in his bed, unable to form a single defiant word, Paul lies in resigned silence. Kitten sees his charge is far gone from him now. He concludes his tale by saying, 'So that was that. I picked up the bicycles and walked home. And now, Paul Latch, I have come back for you.'

The old man's shoulders shudder. It is the first time they have moved in more than a year. They shudder, and the head snaps back viciously, driving out the pillows beneath it. The hard body jerks, and jerks again. The mouth comes open and from it comes a roar. It is a roar such as Kitten has never heard. It is the roar that builds inside after years of life, of injustice, of shame and injury, of sorrow and loss and disappointment and wounded pride and wasted opportunities and willing lies. It is all this and grief – life's grief – anguished by defeat, despite it all. The sound tears through Kitten's sensitive ears, making the demon twins retch. It is the sound of a man who had his own attending devil, which chased him to the end.

Kitten grips the bed sheets, rocks on his toes, clenches shut his eyes, and the sound careers around his head. He feels a dragging pain, a draining deep within himself, for part of him must surely go with Paul, to whom he has devoted a portion of his own existence. He knows, too, the feeling of things being over and well finished, and the release that finality must bring. He opens his eyes while his ears are still ringing, for it is his duty to be watchful until the end.

Paul's head has fallen sideways. In death the stiffness has suddenly left him and Kitten scans the ceiling warily, as if a disease can exist as a floating entity. Already the man is beginning to look lifeless: as Kitten watches, the flesh of the face becomes grey, the sunken cheeks sag further. His eyes, which are open, wipe themselves of their sheen. The black pupils grow rapidly large within their orbs. Death, for Paul Latch, is a thing more active than life.

He'd died unhappy and wrathful, but it was how he'd lived his life, he'd brought this end upon himself. He had lived in the past, so the past had come to live with him. He was not merciful, so mercy could not be granted him. He had not forgiven, so there was no forgiveness. He had never fought his own wickedness, so wickedness fought back at him. He had not escaped his crimes, as no one ever does.

Kitten sighs. He pushes himself away from the bed and drops into the chair. The twins in his head are murmuring a hum. Soon they will go silent, and will remain that way for a long time until one day, when he needs them, they will answer the summons and speak to him.

Outside, evening is coming. The days are growing noticeably shorter. Kitten rubs his face, weary. He must close himself down now, just as the twins are nestling together to slumber in his head. He glances across the room at the corpse and for the first time he feels pity for the old man, and for himself. He had not asked to be sent here, to torment a man for whom he felt nothing, but it was his duty and he'd been given no choice, the task was simply allotted him. History did the allotting, and Paul Latch was doomed long before he knew the name of Kitten Latch. Kitten was called and he came, as his kind must unfailingly do. It was a vendetta, but it was never personal. It is one of the rules: a devil must see the task through, being thorough but never involved. He may accept the aid of those who come to him, but he may enlist the help of none. He may seek out no one for himself, and he must create no binding ties: a devil walks alone. Freedom is vital to a devil. Another rule is this: a devil may expect no rewards. A devil is by nature as powerful as a situation requires: success makes a devil no stronger. A devil has a great capacity for wisdom and learning, and the intelligence to put these things to their best use. In this way the devil gains much – everything, in the end, that a devil needs. The most fiercely underlined rule is this: a devil inhabits the world for others. A devil is the embodiment of wickedness, but a wickedness that turns in on itself, deflecting the evil away from others, repaying the malevolence. A devil is neither good nor bad, right nor wrong: a devil is a reflection, the worm crept out from the heart and soul.

The corpse on the bed is shrinking. In minutes it becomes a poor copy of what it had been. Paul Latch had puffed himself up in life, defiant and proud – how furiously he had fought the sickness that came hand in hand with Kitten's arrival, bellowing at his wife and grandson to accept the blame – but death deflates him, for death likes to haunt a small and cool place. This, too, Kitten knows Paul would rail against, he is a man who would attempt to tyrannise death itself. The thought makes Kitten chuckle: 'Rest, now,' he advises the baleful spirit. 'Let us both, now, have some rest.'

For a time he may live without care, unplagued by immediate concerns. The call will come again for him, he knows, but for the moment he can rest.

Agatha opens the door. She looks at the body, and at her nephew slumped in his chair. 'What happened?' she asks.

Kitten lifts his gaze. 'All I did was tell him a story,' he says.

Agatha goes to the side of the corpse. Kitten watches her inspect the gaunt face. There are no marks on it, no evident signs of violence. 'I'm tired,' he tells her, and there's a complaining, plaintive tone to his voice.

'Yes,' she says, 'I suppose you are.'

'It's been a long day.'

'Go to your room,' she tells him. 'There's things to be done. You're wet and you smell. Go and clean yourself.'

He steps from his chair obediently, and shambles to the door. Agatha pulls the sheet over the face and leaves the room, goes down the hall to the telephone.

An angel has but one purpose in this world, and that is to attend, advise, encourage and caution the devil, and to tidy up when everything is done.

WHEN AIMEE ARRIVES back from work, she is surprised to find that Curtis has beaten her home. 'What's happening?' she asks. 'Is something wrong?'

He's on his knees in the kitchen, pulling saucepans from the shelves and stacking them in boxes. He does not pause or look up at her. 'Did you tell them you wouldn't be resigning?'

'No – Curtis, I'm not going to change my mind. What are you doing?'

'Pack your bags,' he says shortly. 'We're shifting out of here.'

'What?'

He does not repeat his words, and she scans the room. There are other boxes on the table, and she had seen some in the hall. Ptolemy's food bowl is at the top of the rubbish in the bin. She looks back at Curtis and sees that his tracksuit pants are wet and dirty, smearing the linoleum with greyness and black particles. 'Curtis,' she says sharply, 'tell me what's going on.'

'Why should I?' he retorts. 'You've never bothered to tell me what's going on, have you? Hurry up and pack your things, I'm leaving to collect the trailer soon.'

'And where are we going?'

'To my parents' house. They said we could use the bungalow. After that, we'll look for a nice little terrace house. Just what you wanted in the first place, remember? You're going to get your way.'

Aimee shakes her head, incredulous. 'We've only been here two weeks,' she says.

'We won't be staying with my parents for long. Just long enough to get ourselves reorganised. Put the things you'll need there in a separate bag, and everything else in boxes. It'll be easier to load it all straight into the garage.'

'Curtis!' she snaps. 'Stop what you're doing and talk to me!'

He closes the box and looks at her. The bruise on her neck is dark and ugly, but she has done nothing to conceal it. 'Look at you,' he says. 'You look like a whore.'

She catches her breath, astonished. 'I'll tell you what's happened,' he continues. 'I came home early today to sort out that bastard next door.'

'Kitten? What have you done to him?'

'I went over to his place to talk to him. For some reason he wanted to go down to this swampy place. Thought he could confuse me that way, I suppose. I didn't care where the hell I beat the shit out of him.'

'You've hurt him!'

'He's such a poor bloody idiot, I felt sorry for him, is what I did. He's a twit. We go down to this swamp and I was prepared to talk to him rationally. I didn't want him getting hysterical or anything. I told him what I've told him before. Stay away from Aimee, I said. You're really making me lose patience with you.'

He stands up, hefts the box to the table-top. 'He's mad,' he says. 'He's crazy, don't you see? He's a fruit-cake. He said that he wasn't going to leave you alone, that you didn't like me any more, that you've realised I'm not right for you, that you're going to live with him from now on.'

Aimee hears noises from outside, and she darts to the window. She sees that a big dark car has pulled up in the driveway of the house next door, its headlights brightening everything. In the street, another car is parked. She sees one man and then another climb from the big car and skirt its long body. There have never been cars at Kitten's house before.

'You've hurt him,' she whispers.

'I didn't bloody hurt him. He hurt me, more like it. How do you think it felt, hearing all that from some-one like him? I had a right to break his arms, but I didn't.'

'I swear, Curtis, if you've done something terrible to him –'

'He's the one doing terrible things! He's deranged, Aimee. He's getting into your head, twisting your thoughts. He's making you as crazy as he is. It's only a matter of time before something happens that we will really regret, and then I'll be obliged to hurt him. Is that what you want, Aimee?'

The two men have lifted up the rear door of their car and together they slide from it a sleek white and silver form. It is a stretcher bed. 'You have hurt him!' Aimee screams. She spins and rushes at Curtis, and he catches her easily by the wrists.

'What do you expect me to have done?' he asks her. 'Stood there and listened to that? He was laughing at me, I told you! All I did was push him into the water and shake him up a bit. He's perfectly all right. I saw him get on his bike and ride home. Now go to our room and start packing your things. Listen to me! I'm serious about this. I'm not going to have that twerp annoying us every day. Things are difficult enough without that sort of crap distracting me. He's not going anywhere, so we are.'

'You bastard,' she hisses. Her voice is murderous. 'How dare you touch him,' she says. 'How dare you behave like such an animal –'

'I was doing it for you!'

'No, you were not! You've never done anything for me! Everything you do, you do for yourself!'

She's struggling against his grip, and he knows if he releases her she'll fly for his face immediately, with her nails like knives. She is glaring into his eyes, and her own are welling with tears.

'You can do one thing for me,' she says, and her voice is suddenly subdued. 'It's the first and last thing you'll ever need to do. Let me go, Curtis. I'm going, and you are letting me go.'

'Where are you going?'

She stares at him. He is smiling, his words were smug: he does not understand. 'I'm going to Kitten,' she tells him, 'and I'm never coming back. You can keep all this stuff, I won't be needing it.'

He drops her wrists, more from surprise than to grant her freedom. 'You're mad,' he splutters. 'You're as mad as he is. You've only known him two weeks. You hardly know him at all –'

'I know him,' she replies, 'better than I know you.'

As she walks through the house she hears him yelling at her to come back, that she will be back, that she better not think he'll take her back. As she closes the front door he is starting to plead. She slips off her shoes and runs.

At Kitten's house she must stand back from the door, because the men with the stretcher are making their way out. She draws a sharp breath when she sees that the form is enveloped in a bag, that the plastic and the tough zipper reach over the dead face and hide it well from sight. She can only think of Kitten, she does not think of Paul. But Agatha speaks to her, just as she is about to drop to her knees and howl: 'Aimee,' she says, 'Kitten is in his room. Poor Mr Latch, his old heart just stopped. He was such an ill man, for such a long time.'

Aimee clutches at the hand rail, dizzy. She waits impatiently while the men manoeuvre the stretcher through the door and down the stairs, and Agatha and the doctor come out to follow it. Then she steps inside the house, wanting to run but making herself walk, knowing she does not need to leave here again.

Kitten is in his room. For a moment, when she opens the door, she thinks he is sleeping, for he is curled up in his bed. But he opens his blue eyes and lifts his white head and smiles with great kindness at her: 'Good evening, Aimee,' he says.

'Kitten,' she says. 'Kitten, I thought you'd left me.'

'No,' he says. 'It wasn't I who had to leave.'

She comes to him and touches his bare shoulder. 'I'm sorry about your grandfather,' she says.

He lays his head down, against the freshness of his pillow. 'He's gone where he had to go. Everyone does that eventually, as you know.'

'Look what Curtis has done to your face,' she says, softly and sadly, and runs her fingers over the markings on his skin. 'Of all the things he ever did, this is what I could never forgive him for.'

'Tell me,' says Kitten, 'have you decided?'

'You knew there never really was a choice,' she replies.

He smiles, and wraps his hand around her tickling fingers. 'From now on,' he says, 'you can make all the choices you like. I will never tell you what to do. I'll never tell you what to think or where to go or how you must behave.'

She is nervous, made shy by the knowledge that they

belong to each other now, and she laughs awkwardly. 'Maybe I'll grow feathers,' she suggests, 'and then I can fly. Like your bird. Like an angel.'

'Like an angel,' he agrees.

'And I can really stay with you? I can really go to the country, with you? I'm afraid, Kitten,' she says. 'This future frightens me.'

He does not tell her one needn't fear the future, but only the past. He pushes the covers down for her and she climbs in beside him. The bed is warm, and his body is clean, and she feels instantly drowsy. He puts an arm around her and it is a pleasure such as she's never known, the languid warmth, the closeness of him, the realisation that she no longer knows how she will live out her days. She'd once asked who he was and what he was doing, and she sees now that he was sent to show her all she had and all she did not need, a being come to earth specially for her.

She closes her eyes and snuggles closer to him. She hears Agatha shut the front door and the neat sliding of the bolt, and hears with this the promise of living happily ever after.

Part two

THEY HAVE BEEN living in this place for a year, and in the town their faces are known.

People assume Kitten and Aimee to be brother and sister: they share similar colouring, the fair hair, the light eyes. They are distant to each other in public, and distant to the public: no one would say they are gregarious souls although Aimee, alone, will be gracious and friendly. Agatha could be their grandmother, though people have heard enough to know she is Aunt. None of the three appears to have an occupation but they are never short of money, and Agatha gives generously to local fundraisers and fêtes.

They live, the three of them, in a small house on the outskirts of the town. It is an old house, made of wood: under its floorboards snakes sometimes shelter, and possums amble up and down the corrugated roof. All around the house are trees and fields of long, startlingly green grass. Behind the house runs a creek studded with stepping-stones and jumping with tadpoles. Soon after they arrived they started a vegetable patch and a flower garden, for which they bought plants and seeds. The cockatoo began to grow feathers and Kitten gave up his cigarettes.

The gravelled road that leads to the house is not a busy one, and little traffic breaks the serenity of each day. The trees are filled with wild birds and Aimee, for fun, has built a scarecrow. From the back veranda, made dreamy by the aroma of bread and the heat of the sun, she watches the scarecrow spin against the breeze and wonders why she wasted so many years doing anything but this. She looks back with pride at her courage and daring: it is no small thing, to change one's life, and yet now she has done so, it seems a thing hardly worth mentioning. It was something she was born to do, is all.

It is March, and the weather is fine.

Kitten is in the garden. He likes to be outside with the sun on his skin, although if it is hot he will burn. He has skirted the house with a vast semicircle of garden, planting it with shrubs and roses and his favourites, oleander. At first he had been able to work the earth only an hour or two before falling down exhausted, but he has grown stronger and healthier and now he can work all day if he wishes, eating his lunch with one hand and driving a spade with the other. He uses the tools he once kept locked in a garden shed. He was at first cautious and uncertain with them, struggling with their weight and correct method of use, but now he wields them with skill and authority. The vegetable patch yields more than the three of them can eat and from any of the front or side windows they can look out and see their fortress of foliage and flowers.

A black fly is bothering him, attracted by the activity and the dampness of his skin. For a time he ignores it, for he is busy planting daffodil bulbs. When they come up in winter he will cut them for Aimee, and put them in a vase where she can see them when she wakes. He is clever at guessing what will please her, and he wishes the bulbs would hurry and grow. From this distance he can hear her, talking to Agatha in the kitchen. Aimee, too, has grown strong and healthy here. She gets about barefooted, and travels alone on long walks. He doesn't ask where she goes, and never asks to go with her. Sometimes she takes Agatha along, and Agatha says she goes nowhere in particular, just around. Agatha tells Kitten that Aimee is devoted to him, says she sees it shining in the girl's blue eyes. At night Aimee curls up close to him and he feels her breath on his chest. Because they are happy, Agatha too is happy. She tells Kitten she can't believe how well things have turned out, how lucky she is to be here.

Kittens straightens, and wipes a grubby wrist across his eyes. The fly darts away and returns immediately, desperate to be allowed to settle. He whispers a warning to it under his breath. He hears Agatha say something about calling him for lunch, and he has bulbs that need planting while the earth is still cool. He tosses his head as the fly comes near, and the insect artfully veers. Impatient, Kitten's hands snap together to dispatch it in the air, and they miss. The startled fly careers downwards, somersaults, catches the air and vanishes. Kitten stares at his empty hands, which have never missed a thing.

The demon twins have not spoken to him since the moment Paul Latch died. He has not missed their company, but without them he is getting slow.

'Kitten!' calls Aimee, and he looks up from his hands. She is standing on the front veranda, leaning against the railing. Her hair is cut short now, and the wind buffets it about. Close to her the cockatoo is perched, its crested head craned sideways as it dozes in the sunshine. It is not kept in a cage any more, but it never flies away. 'Wash your hands and come inside,' Aimee commands. 'It's time for lunch.'

He nods and waves at her, leaves the bulbs and spade where they lie, and follows the garden hose until it brings him to the tap.

Lately he has begun to miss Aimee. It seems such a long time since he's seen her – much longer than a year. He remembers her laughter, for she always liked to laugh. She would make jokes that baffled him, while greatly amusing herself. She laughed like a kid, boisterously. Sometimes she'd laugh until he wanted to throttle her, and then he'd find himself reluctantly beginning to giggle.

He takes out albums and flips through them, smiling each time he sees her face. She was always lovely, that pale skin and those thin limbs, she looked like she would never grow old. He has pictures of her when she was a child and he wishes he knew better what those days were like for her: so much of history is lost. Aimee herself is lost. A year ago she walked away from everything she knew. Calmly, blithely, she simply walked away. He will never see her when she grows old, she'll never tell him what it was like for her to be young. He wants to ask her many things about herself, what she's thinking, where she will go. He thinks he must be growing sentimental, wanting so badly to see her again.

Everyone knows Aimee has disappeared, possibly for good. She's gone off with people she hardly knew. It surprised everyone, not least himself. But, he thinks, if he looked for her, he'd find her. She's not hiding: she's just gone.

One warm March day he is driving, busy on some errand for his work, and finds his mind is wandering. He slows the car to a cruise. Then he hits the brake and turns the car around. Close to here is the place where Aimee and Curtis once lived.

He recognises the house as soon as he sees it, for a year has made little difference. There's a toppled child's tricycle in the front garden, and when he steps from the car he hears music coming from within. He lights a cigarette and looks around. The street is empty and, except for the music, quiet. He crosses the road and stops on the footpath, looking not at Aimee's house, but at the house next door. It was here that the people lived, the people Aimee ran with.

The curtains are drawn over the front windows, and the weeds in the garden are long. An empty house can never conceal its vacantness, and this house has been empty for a year. He takes another look around, and no one is looking back at him, so he walks up the driveway and into the backyard. There's nothing to see but grass and weeds and plants and trees; there's a garden shed with its door pushed back hard. He peeps inside and sees empty benches, spiderwebs.

He tries the screen door of the house, which is open, but the wooden door beyond it is locked. He tests several windows and none of them will budge. But this is a safe neighbourhood, its very dullness keeps it undisturbed. The security belongs to an older, less menacing world, when a bolt across the door was defence enough. He soon finds a place that will let him in. He removes the glass plates from the bathroom's louvre windows and, standing on an overturned bucket, he hoists himself inside.

The house smells musty, and he thinks he hears something scurry. There's no furniture, and nothing on the walls but clean patches where pictures once hung. The tap in the kitchen is dripping and it has stained the stainless steel.

There's nothing for him in the lounge room or the dining room, and he wonders what he's searching for. There are three doors leading off the hallway and he opens the furthest one. This is a small room, utterly empty. The next room is empty. The next room, empty again. It makes him feel bested, the thorough way they've cleaned out this place: it is as if they suspected he would one day come prying. And it makes him angry, too: by removing all sign of themselves, they've erased Aimee as well.

It's quiet enough for him to hear his watch ticking, and he looks down to check the time. He is late, he's due back at work any moment now. There's nothing here, but it's here that he makes a decision: he'll find her, to show them that he can. She's not hiding, but he won't have them thinking they've successfully spirited her away.

He leaves the house as he found it, but something leaves with him, gliding through the window as he puts the last of the glass back into its place. It is the smell of age and disuse and dampness that follows him, and when it reaches the fresh air it does not disperse but lingers, as if uncertain of which direction it wishes to go.

Kitten pulls the chair out and sits down. 'Hands clean?' asks Aimee and, frowning, he shows her his palms. His hair is tied with a bandanna which she removes, ruffling free the locks until they look the way she likes them. He waves her hand away and she laughs, leans forward to kiss his ear.

Agatha has made ham sandwiches and cut them into squares. 'That's how my mother used to cut bread when we were kids,' Aimee tells her, and the old woman smiles. Kitten takes one and holds it up to the light: it seems too small and silly to eat, and he puts it down again.

'Stay out of the sun this afternoon, Kitten,' Agatha tells him. 'Look, you're already starting to burn.'

'Aimee,' he says, pointing at her notepad, 'what is that you've written?'

Aimee hesitates: Kitten does not like her to dwell on the subject of her family. 'I never want to know,' he's told her, 'about anything from your past,' and this applies to deeds done as well as people known. He is grieved and sulky when she mentions a thing, so she says little, at least to him, and when phoning home she is brief and evasive, for he is usually lingering nearby. 'It's just – a quick note – to my mum.'

'Lovely, sweetie. What does it say?' Agatha, too, fears Aimee's past: she knows she is party to the abduction of this child.

'. . . Nothing, really. That the weather is fine. That Kitten has made a pretty garden.'

'Aren't you good,' muses Kitten, 'writing a letter. I haven't got anyone to write to . . . Agatha, that's true, isn't it? There's no one in the world I could write to, even if I wanted to.'

'What about your school friends?'

'I hated my school friends.'

Hated . . . hated . . . friends. Kitten hears the words as a scratching in his mind. With them comes a slight pain, as if something prickly has gripped his shoulder to bring itself to his attention.

'You almost never went to school, if I remember clearly. Not when he was a little boy, he was home as often as anywhere. Mr Latch would come in one door and Kitten would dart out the other, forever trying to hide himself.'

Aimee, unlike Kitten, loves to hear about the past, but he is reticent and rarely tells her anything: most of what she knows has been learned in snippets from Agatha. She suspects he is embarrassed by his life, ashamed that his parents did not want to keep him and he had to be reared by grudging, grizzled relatives. She wants so much for him to feel otherwise, for it pains her that he carries this wound. 'My life has been ordinary, but your life has been remarkable,' she once told him, to encourage and please him, and he had replied darkly, 'Your life has been remarkably ordinary, and my life has only been ordinarily remarkable.'

Now she asks Agatha, 'Why didn't you make him go to school?'

Agatha shrugs, and puts a plate of sliced cake on the table. 'What for?' she says. 'He was clever enough for me. They sent a man around to see me once, to ask me why I didn't make him go. I think Kitten was about ten.'

'What did you say?'

'I said, He knows everything a ten-year-old boy needs to know. When he's eleven, I'll send him back to you.'

Aimee cocks her head, suspecting a joke, and Agatha winks jauntily at her. They like to tease each other, and

Aimee turns to Kitten. 'Is that true?' she asks. 'Did you really never go to school?'

Not never. Not forever. The words are not clear, they sound as if spoken through gravel, and they hurt. Kitten sits still in his chair, but the hairs on his arms stand up. Agatha is laughing. 'It's not good,' she's saying, 'for a naughty boy to know too much.'

'Shut up,' hisses Kitten. 'For a moment, would you please shut up . . .'

Agatha and Aimee blink at him. He puts his head in his hands and digs his nails into his skin. 'Kitten,' says Aimee, 'what's the matter?'

'He's been in the sun too long, it's given you a headache, hasn't it?'

'It's not hot, I've been out there myself . . .'

'Have a rest,' advises Agatha. 'The garden will be there tomorrow.'

Kitten says nothing. He had thought for a moment that the voice belonged to the twins, but he realises that is a desperate hope. He remembers the twins, the sound of them, the feel of them. This pain is not familiar, and comes from nothing vaguely like the sun.

He pushes out his chair and stands. 'May I please be excused?'

'Kitten –'

'Kitten, don't be foolish, the garden can wait, you haven't eaten –'

'No,' he says. 'No, you don't understand.'

He goes to the door and as he hurries down the hall

he hears Aimee call his name, and Agatha advising her to leave him be.

By the time he reaches the garden he is panicked and the pressure in his skull makes him stagger. He stumbles to the tap and turns it on so hard that the gushing water breaks up the earth below. Mud leaps in droplets to his trousers and his arms, and burrs in the grass stick into his knees. The pain in his head tightens, turns over, tightens again. He presses his dripping hands to his face and closes his eyes against the voice. *Kitten*, it says: *Kitten Latch. Are you hearing me?*

That night he writes a list of the possible ways he might find her. She has given them no phone number and no address. Occasionally she makes a phone call and tells them she's all right, but she never tells them where she's calling from. She must know no one approves of this strange and wilful thing she's done. She no doubt fears they think she's caught in something cultish and that what they'd like is to drag her forcibly away. So she is guarded, when she calls, and says only what she wants them to know.

But he has no intention of dragging her away. He just wants to look at her and hear her laugh again. He wants to assure himself that she's really safe, that she's as happy as she always claims to be. And if he finds that this is so, he's quite prepared to leave her be. He's come to think that life is short and people should be allowed to live as they wish. It's not so awful, as long as she's happy. And he's come to think just one other thing, which applies to Aimee in particular: that perhaps she's best off where she is, that maybe she's not fit to be anywhere else.

How do you find someone when you don't know where they are?

ARE YOU HEARING ME?

Kitten opens his eyes and sits up, uncertain what has woken him. Aimee is sleeping quietly beside him and he thinks that perhaps a truck has passed on the road outside. Maybe the wind has rattled the old house, maybe a branch has fallen from a tree.

No no no.

'Yes,' he says, 'I know.'

Aimee stirs and he looks down at her. A wisp of hair flutters on her cheek as she breathes, and he wipes the strands away. He steps from the bed and tucks the blankets around her shoulders. He moves carefully, wary of the pain the voice brought with it that afternoon. He has a dressing-gown and he slips it over himself, leaving his feet bare. The house has no curtains and the rooms are lit by the moon, he finds his way easily to the kitchen. The voice follows him, saying nothing, but he knows it is with him for there is a faint crackling, crumbling sound, like something digging itself out of the earth. He opens the back door and looks into the night. In the moonbeams he can see the scarecrow: there is a breeze, it is strong, and it makes the scarecrow seem agitated and alive. Everything else looks foreign, lit up in black and white, but the scarecrow looks alive.

He needs to ask a hundred questions. 'Who are you?' he whispers. 'What do you want?'

The crackling grows momentarily louder, and fades away again. Kitten waits, watching the scarecrow shudder. Eventually he repeats, 'What do you want?'

For long minutes there is nothing. He taps his foot on the lino floor. He feels the voice struggling and failing and finally he sighs. 'I cannot hear you,' he says. 'I feel you, but I can't hear you. You're faint –'

I feel you, answers the voice. It is distant and it sounds as if it, like the treetops, is being pummelled by the wind, yet it makes Kitten draw a sharp breath.

'You hurt,' he says. 'You may not know it, but you damage me when you speak. You must be careful. I will listen to you, but please take care.'

The voice says nothing. The wind flicks Kitten's hair and tugs the hem of his gown. It rattles the calendar against the wall, flips the pages of the newspaper, yanks the bills off the refrigerator, shakes the window in its frame. The kitchen is loud and vibrant with the invasion. Kitten stands his ground. He has been found. His time of resting is over. He looks out at the darkness and it is easy to believe he stands at the end of everything, that this hollow moment is all that's left, its origins traceable through billions of years to the beginning ball of energy and flame.

'Twins?' he asks.

Twins? Twins?

'I am Latch,' Kitten declares, across the empty fields. 'Don't touch me. Don't come near me. I do not fear you. You will not win.'

I am Latch, echoes the voice. *I am Latch, you will not win.*

He goes to the house where his mother and father live and after coffee and light conversation he searches through the cartons full of things she left behind. He supposes he will find no important clue inside them, for the boxes have been gone through time and time again, but nonetheless he tips the contents over the carpet. Aimee has abandoned all her books, all her toys, all the trinkets she'd collected over the years. He finds Christmas cards, makeup, burned-down candles, cookery tools. He finds a quaint wind-up puppy dog he'd given her as a birthday present, and this saddens him. She had always been a sentimental girl, devoted to friends and family, she'd kept all the little foolish things that meant nothing, a second-place ribbon she'd won in a race, a concert ticket, a bow-shaped twig someone had put in her hair. In the boxes he finds these things that gave Aimee a sense of history. Seeing them, he feels her loss as if she's died.

His mother has come into the room and she looks at the clutter on the floor. 'I don't know what to do with the clothes,' she tells him. 'I don't want to throw them away, in case she wants them again one day.'

113

'Don't throw them away,' he says. 'Don't throw anything away.'

'But it seems pointless to keep them –'

'She's not dead,' he says firmly. 'She'll come back one day. You have to think of it as if she's gone on holiday somewhere. Look at this stuff: look how much she loved everyone –'

'But she left it behind.'

'But she didn't throw it away. That must mean she'll be back for it one day.'

The mother considers this, flipping idly through the pages of a book of nursery rhymes. She closes the book and sighs. 'What are you searching for?' she asks.

'I don't know . . . something that might tell us where she is.'

'You won't find anything.'

'Something I don't recognise . . . a hint . . .'

'There's nothing. I've been through it a hundred times.'

'Hmm.' He sits on his haunches and ponders. A jar of face cream is rocking on the carpet, unbalanced by the fountain pen lodged beneath it. Aimee was a girl who always made herself up carefully, who liked expensive clothes and took care of herself. Has she gone, then, to a place where the way she looks doesn't matter any more?

'I'm going to find her,' he says. 'If she's happy, I'm not going to make her come back. But at least we'll know, then, that she's all right.'

The mother hugs the book to her chest. 'I want her back,' she says.

'I know, but she's grown up now. You can't make her do something she doesn't want to do. If we know she's happy, that's better than knowing nothing. And if she sees we're not going to drag her away, she might let us visit her sometimes, or she might come to visit us. We have to do this carefully.'

'I suppose so,' his mother reluctantly agrees.

'If you find anything, will you tell me? There's nothing here, but something might turn up.'

Aimee sits on the back veranda: it is her favourite place. From here she can see the peppercorn trees that jostle each other for a position by the creek. She likes these trees, with their gnarled twisting branches and their leaves that look lacy and benign from a distance and are pointed like knives up close. She'd not known they were called peppercorn – Kitten told her this – and she likes the pretty name as well. Kitten amazes her with the things he knows, and what he tells her she remembers better than anything she was ever taught at school. He hasn't taught her to write letters, however, and she's as bad at this as she's always been. The letter has many crossed-out words and lines, things she's scribbled because they were spelled wrong or sounded idiotic. Whole pages have been pulled from the notebook and lie in disgrace at her feet, crumpled into balls. She thinks it is a waste of time, and knows that

Kitten disapproves of the idea, but she also knows how much pleasure it will give her mother to receive a letter, and once the fancy was in her head she could not make it leave.

Let me tell you how we spend our days, she writes. *Agatha is always up earliest, and when I wake up I always smell tea and honey toast, it is so delicious. Sometimes I lie in bed especially so I can smell it for longer. Agatha is a fantastic cook – I think I will get very fat! After breakfast I have a shower and the hot water doesn't last long so I'm usually colder when I get out than when I got in, but I'm used to that now. After that there's nothing much to do but please don't think I'm bored, or being lazy, because neither of that is true. I love just sitting around, looking at the trees, watching the sun go up and down. We do whatever we want to do. Some days I clean the house. It is a cute house, really old. It has a bomb shelter! With concrete walls! It used to be the cellar, I think. It is spooky. We found newspapers and really old tins of jam in there. Kitten used it in summer (the bomb shelter, not the jam) when he made some beer. It was disgusting (the beer). Living like this is much better than going to work, coming home, going to work . . . It makes me sad, to think of how I used to do that every day.*

She lowers her pen and bites her lip. She wants to find the words that will make her mother happy, for she knows how fretful she must be. Aimee looks up, shading her eyes against the sun. In the distance she can see Kitten crouched in the grass, his hands on his knees. He's wearing a tatty singlet, and has a straw hat on his head.

My friend Kitten is in the paddock as I write this. He is sitting down and he's very still – there must be something in the grass, a skink or some funny insect – I hope it is not a snake! I don't like snakes. Kitten is a strange person – I suppose Curtis has told you that, and you wonder what it means. It means that he's not like anyone I've ever met. He knows everything about animals and plants. Lots of things are interesting to him, like a lizard in the grass, the way a kid would be interested in things like that.

She pauses, struggling for words. She lifts her gaze, nibbles the end of her pen. Kitten has not moved. She wants to find words that will do him justice, that will make her parents trust and like him. And yet, over the year, there have been times when she has not trusted him, when she's downright disliked him. He can be impatient, demanding, sour. He is not always predictable: he can laugh when she is serious, take offence when she jokes. He likes to have his way and will endure no interference. He falls into depressions that last hours or days. His thoughts consume him sometimes, and everything becomes nothing to him then. He can be easily bored, easily frustrated, easily provoked. His temper can be fierce.

From his place in the grass he looks around at her, as if he's heard the things she's thinking. She waves quickly, and he smiles at her from under the brim of his hat. None of his faults were known to her when she decided to come here with him, but she has never wanted to leave because of them. If she is made angry and disappointed by him, she needs only to wait: he hauls himself out of his storminess, full of apology and remorse, and he belongs to her again, then, her clever, cheerful, charming Kitten, she's always overjoyed to have him back. She gazes at him thoughtfully, and puts her pen to the page.

I love him so much, she writes, *that sometimes I love just looking at him.* This seems enough. It's easy to end the letter now.

Please don't worry about me, Mum. This is a great place to live. I do not have a job yet and Kitten and Agatha tell me not to worry about it. They have inherited a lot of money and we live off that. I feel a bit bad about this, but I do what I can to earn my keep. They tell me I do this by just being here and being their friend.

She reads what she's written, not completely content with it, but knowing it's the best she can do. She signs her name and puts under it a dozen crossed kisses. She folds the pages in half and goes inside to find an envelope.

The voice is struggling. He listens to it closely, withstanding the pain it causes him. Nothing about it is making sense. It fades in and out of clarity like a radio fraught with interference and weak frequency. For long periods of time it is silent, or buzzes erratically to itself. He knows it is not the twins for although the twins could be a torment they were there to assist him, and they had known their place. They had often disagreed with him, but they resignedly went along with the decisions he made. They did not have independence. They had gnashing teeth and razors on their toes and they could hurt him when they wanted to, but they were allies. He longs to hear their snarling voices now, for he feels alone. He has a creeping and unpleasant suspicion that there is no longer room for them in his head. The voice has forced them out and taken their place.

Latch, it says: *Latch.*

What are you? he asks. He's learned he does not need to speak the words aloud.

Latch?

Until you have the strength to speak clearly, leave me be.

He feels how this irritates the voice, for it knows and hates that it is weak. Kitten is reminded of a foal trying to stand, falling on its face, trying again.

You will not . . . You will not . . .

Oh, I will not what?

You will not be left alone.

He drops his gaze, plucks the grass around his knees. Sweat is dampening his forehead and he wipes it away. He is reluctant to seem disturbed.

I am the devil Latch, he says. I am stronger than you.

You don't know what I am.

Compared to me, you are nothing.

The voice hums smugly. 'Twins,' Kitten whispers, scarcely saying the word, hoping to sneak the summons through.

No twins. Latch. Latch.

'God, I hate you,' Kitten mutters, vexed.

Ha ha. Ha ha.

Tell me what you want.

Revenge. Latch breaks devil law.

Kitten feels as if a knife has skimmed up his spine. What law?

You know.

No.

Yes.

Tell me.

Devil walks the world alone.

Kitten looks over his shoulder then, to where Aimee sits on the veranda, writing her letter. She waves to him, and he smiles grimly at her from under his hat.

Yes, says the voice, *Latch knows. Devil walks the world alone.*

She does no harm. She's a girl, she doesn't harm.

Latch is no devil if Latch breaks devil law.

Kitten forces his teeth together. You insult me. You waste my time. You annoy me like a flea. You know nothing. You are ignorant and feeble and boring.

'Twins!' Kitten barks.

Latch yelps like a mongrel. Twins! Twins!

Leave me, I order you!

A devil walks alone.

I need her.

Devil walks alone.

I hate you.

I hate you. You break the natural law.

'Stick it,' says Kitten, 'up your arse.'

The voice falls into a glowering silence. Kitten, exhausted and sagging in the grass, manages to laugh. He is beginning to suspect what the voice might be and soon he will be made to respect it but for the moment, while it struggles, he can laugh. He is a devil, and it does not become a devil to show fear.

At the dinner table that night he studies her under his lashes. Eventually he lays his cutlery down and leans forward in his chair. 'Aimee,' he says, 'what would you do, if you had to leave here?'

She shrugs carelessly, not looking up from her meal. 'I don't know. Go where you go, I guess.'

'No. If you had to leave without us, where would you go?'

Her knife and fork slump in her hands. 'What do you mean?' she asks, and glances worriedly at Agatha. 'Why would that happen?'

'It's only a question.'

'Kitten,' Agatha warns.

'Do you want me to leave?'

'You don't have to go anywhere, sweetie. You can stay here as long as you like. Kitten is fussing over nothing.'

He shoots a black glance at his aunt. 'I am not fussing. Can't I ask a question?'

'Well what is the point of it, Kitten?'

'I was wondering, nothing else.'

Aimee stares at him and he looks closely at her, his blue eyes scanning her face. She falters, unnerved. He has never put the query to her before, and everything inside her has gone cold. 'I'd go . . . home, I suppose.'

'You don't want to?'

'No . . . you know that, Kitten.'

'But it pleases me, to know you have somewhere to go if you had to.'

Aimee looks around the kitchen, and there's desperation in her gaze. 'I'm happy here,' she mutters. 'I never want to leave.'

'No one can be happy forever.'

'Kitten –'

'If you want me to leave, just say so!'

She pushes back her chair and stalks from the room. Kitten looks at Agatha, who is frowning fiercely at him. She says, 'You're mean, Kitten Latch.'

He picks up his fork and stabs a small potato. 'I wanted to know.'

'To know what? That she loves you? Do you need to be told?'

'Maybe it's important to me, Agatha.'

Agatha shakes her head. She finds it difficult to be angry with him. He looks deceptively calm as he sits there, but she has known him well for a long time: she knows his moodiness, and she knows when there is something worse. She asks, 'What's been bothering you, this last couple of days?'

He turns the fork between his fingers, and the potato skids through gravy. For a time he is solemnly silent. Then he pushes back his plate and sighs. 'Something's going to happen,' he tells her, 'and I'm not certain what it is.'

She nods, understanding this. 'Don't look too far ahead,' she advises. 'Live day by day. Things seem worse, if you look ahead. Nothing is ever what you expected when you finally get there. Go and get some rest. Worrying wears a person out.'

He lifts his eyes and smiles at her. Her wisdom, he knows, is cheap, meaningless, and ultimately useless. But, 'You have always been a good and wise friend to me,' he says, and surprises her by leaning across the table to kiss her cheek. He leaves the kitchen, then, to find Aimee and be contrite, to wipe her tears if she's crying, to jolly her into grudging laughter if she's cross, to promise her his questions meant nothing. Agatha, watching him go, longs to run after him. She wants to squeeze him, hide him, tell him that nothing will ever touch him because she would stop it first, with her life, but she lets him go. Such a declaration would embarrass him, and make him angry and sad.

I HAVE BEEN THINKING.

Strike up the band.

I think I know who you are.

Oh?

Everything that is natural must have its natural parent. Isn't that what you are to me?

I own you, true.

You've always been with me, haven't you? Even when I didn't know you were there, there you were.

Kitten wasn't wanted by anyone else. Wiped away like dust, like dirt.

No one else has ever mattered. I did not need any other parent, because I have you. I've always thought you must exist. But I cannot understand why you wish to hurt me.

Latch breaks devil law.

You are painful.

You are wrong.

I have always done what I had to do. I have never complained. I have never expected a reward. I have done everything to the best of my ability. Can I not have something that pleases me, in this long life?

No.

You are unreasonable.

You are devil.

I am alone.

As devil must be.

Kitten stamps a foot against the earth. You are not here. You do not endure what I endure. You make a devil, and then you abandon. You have no right to tell me what I must and must not do.

The blow hits him under the chin and throws him to the ground. For a moment he lies dazed, his mind spinning, his vision blacked. He draws a breath and sits up on his elbows, surprised to find everything about him exactly as it had been. The grass is tatty and flattened, beaten down by the wind. The house is sitting squat some distance away, guarded by its garden.

Feel that, Kitten?

Kitten nods dumbly. He has bitten his tongue and tastes blood in his mouth.

I can do what I wish to you.

He wipes his face, nods again.

The pompous one is not so noisy now.

. . . You should not harm me.

You are mine. Say so.

Kitten lies in the dirt. He can feel the voice waiting, growing impatient. It buzzes in the air, spinning through his flesh and ears.

Latch! Say the words!

Kitten's jaw aches. There is no mark there, the blow will not leave a bruise, yet it had hurt and hurts still.

I am yours.

Who am I?

The one that makes the devil. The one that watches. The one that makes the law.

Get on your knees.

Kitten blinks and stares. Around him is nothing but the empty countryside, the trees.

On your knees.

No, I will not –

Be humble, Latch! Your insolence has always been nauseating to me, I will have no more of it! You should be honoured I have sought you out. Must I make you obey? On your knees.

Kitten pushes himself to his feet, and kneels down in the grass.

Ask me to pardon your insulting behaviour.

Forgive me.

I do not think I can. Say you are wrong. Say you are a fool. Remember my touch!

. . . I am wrong. I have been foolish.

How I laugh, to look at you. Proud Latch!

Kitten grinds his teeth. As you are who you are, what is it you wish me to do?

Kitten Latch is pathetic. Fool, fool –

Stop! It achieves nothing, to torment me in this way! You would take from me what little I have: must you also debase and abuse me? What do you wish me to do? If I must walk alone, I will walk alone –

I care not what you do.

Kitten, confused, hesitates, lifting his eyes to the sky. It cares not what I do. The entity is potent, but it lacks reason. Its superior tone is not the tone of the truly superior. Its thoughts flit in a manner untypical of a great power. It forgets, it disregards, it postures, it has no brilliance behind it. He looks down at the grass, feels the sun's warmth in the earth beneath his feet.

Latch is mine. I do as I please.

You are cruel to the ones you create.

I care for nothing I create.

That is not the natural way, Kitten replies coolly. I do not understand you, your actions make no sense.

I need not make sense. I do as I please.

I will do as you want, but first you must prove you are the one you claim to be. Surely something as supreme as the natural parent has no call for underhand blows, or would be weak, as you once were? If you cannot prove yourself, how can I obey you? Why should I trust you? Why listen? Why –

Latch! Be silent! Cunning Latch, you are right, I am not what makes devil. I am like you: I am what is sent. I am punishment. I am revenge. Latch is mine. Latch breaks law, so Latch is given to me. I am Paul. Remember me? Remember me? Remember me?

When the mother receives the letter, she weeps. It makes her cry to see Aimee's handwriting, the careful crossing and dotting of the letters. She presses the pages to her face, wanting to touch something her daughter has touched, as if she can feel the kisses.

She reads the letter over and over. She searches for a message between the lines. She strains to see what her child has been unable to put down: she looks for fear, loneliness, unhappiness, desperation. But what she finds is a simple letter from someone who sounds content – indeed, joyful. And this makes the mother weep.

Aimee's father agrees that there's nothing they can do. Their daughter has made a decision and they will gain nothing from treating her like something that needs to be told. People lose their offspring forever by doing that. 'Aimee's an adult, after all,' he says.

The mother looks at her husband with despair and a trace of loathing. Her blood is chilled with all she has lost. 'She's still a baby to me,' she answers. 'She'll always be a little girl to me.'

She rings her son and he comes over, and together they scan the letter. 'Look,' says the mother. 'She hasn't put her address on it. She doesn't want me to write back. She doesn't want to be found.'

'Maybe she just forgot.'

'She didn't forget.'

'She's written you a letter. She doesn't want you to forget her. That's a start.'

'She doesn't want us to find her, though.'

'She's made a mistake, then. Maybe she made it on purpose. Look at the envelope. What does it say?'

The mother snatches up the envelope. There, over and obscured by the stamp, is a circular mark placed there by a post-office employee to say that the letter is paid for and legal, and started its journey in a town that can be found on any map.

'Can you read it?' he asks. 'Are the letters clear?'

'Yes, they're clear.'

She reads them out and he writes them down. They look at the word that has been formed. 'Hello, Aimee,' he says. 'We thought we'd lost you.'

At dinner that evening Aimee says, 'My letter would have arrived today.'

Agatha smiles at her. She is relieved the girl has forgiven Kitten his testing enquiry, apparently with ease. She suspects her loyalty will always lie with her naughty Kitten, but she is fond enough of Aimee for it to be disappointing, to have her go. They make an odd but cosy family here. And the girl has given Kitten grounding, something Agatha knows he's never had. Aimee, too, smiles, to herself. It pleases her, how pleased her mother will be with the offering from her child.

They are having pasta for dinner and Agatha brings a great steaming plate of it to the table. Her arthritic hands are bundled into oven gloves. 'Kitten,' she says, 'pass your bowl.'

He looks up at her, frowning.

'Your bowl?'

He pushes the bowl towards his aunt, and looks

back down at the tablecloth. A pattern of shamrock has been sewn into it, and the creases of folds make ridges along the material.

Tell me the story, I must know.

Do not order me, wretch.

Now that he knows it is Paul, he is not so cautious. This is something with which he is acquainted.

Don't you wish to tell me about yourself?

The voice buzzes, thinking this over. Kitten knows it will be forthcoming: Paul was vain and liked to talk about himself.

'This looks really delicious,' Aimee says, but Agatha mutters disgruntledly.

'I don't like that butcher,' she grumbles. 'I think his mince is fatty.'

There is no story. I have come to you, as you once came to me. Now the devil has a devil.

But someone must have sent you.

The same that sent you. What you know, I know.

So you have not met the natural parent, either. For all we know, we know little, wouldn't you agree?

'I was under the impression that one gets better quality food in the country. I must say, I haven't seen the proof so far. Cheese?'

Aimee shakes her head, and Agatha proffers the cheese to Kitten.

'Kitten? Eat, before it gets cold.'

He hears the old woman distantly, and takes up his fork.

You live well, off the money I made.

Yes, we do.

My money.

Ah, Pauly, you have no use for it now.

Respect me, brat. Remember who I am. Recall how you feared me when I was man. I will rule you. As when you were a child, Kitten. Remember me?

But you are no longer man. You are something new. And I have been what I am for a very long time. I am good, at being what I am. Even when I was young, I was a superior thing to you. You are only Paul.

Aimee sucks in a strand of pasta and dabs her mouth with a napkin. 'When I was in town posting the letter,' she says, 'I saw a sign advertising puppies being given away. Do you think we should get a dog?'

You have been given to me to do with as I please. You have broken the law and I may punish as I desire. I understand and obey my duty. Unlike you.

I will not give her up. You do not frighten me. Rant and rave as much as you like, you worry me less than do the birds in the trees. Now tell me, Paul, what was it like to die, to be dead? You liked to tell me things, while you were alive. Indeed, you never missed an opportunity to impart your knowledge to me, regardless of whether or not I wished to hear it. Won't you do so now?

No.

Please. Your experience is beyond me, and of infinite worth.

The voice withdraws, considering. In the silence Agatha says, 'Well, I think it's a fine idea. Kitten, what do you think?'

To die is to be peeled. Death is life in layers. To be cleaved like a loaf, to wrap around space –

'Kitten?'

He lifts his head sharply, annoyed by the distraction. 'What?' he growls.

'Aimee wants to get a dog.'

'A gorgeous little puppy. Oh, think of it, a puppy would be so cute. Please say yes.'

You'll know death intimately when I am done with you, Latch.

Agatha clicks her tongue impatiently. 'Kitten, why aren't you eating? I thought you liked pasta.'

'Don't waste it, Kitten –'

'I'm not hungry,' he says, and his mind is taxed with the effort of finding the words, of coping with a life that is like death, layered. 'Why are you always forcing food into me? Is it so important? I'm tired of this endless, endless food.'

I will drain the animation from you. I will leave a fragile husk. I will take everything you think you have. You will do and say what I wish of you.

You make me laugh. How did you die, Paul? Who was there to witness it? Who saw your eyes lose their sheen? Who heard death blast through your frozen body? Remember me?

Aimee reaches over and tugs at his sleeve. 'Anyway,

what do you say, Kitten? This is a farm, sort of, and we need a dog.'

Now all is changed. Already you are growing weak. You will grow weaker still. Look, you upset your aunt, you do not eat. What, then, are you doing with that fork?

Kitten feels a jolting, sickening pain in his right hand. He hasn't a chance to look at the injury because he turns to Aimee and shouts, 'No, I don't want a dog! I hate dogs! Dogs hate me! You're not to get a dog!'

Aimee and Agatha fall back in their chairs, horrified. Kitten feels the terrible pain and looks down to see the prongs of the fork buried deep in his palm. His left hand is tight around the length of the instrument, clenched as if never to let go.

Ha ha.

Kitten is shocked and white. His tired mind reels. He stares at the embedded fork, hopelessly unable to decide what should be done. It seems a long time before Agatha gets up from her chair and unfurls his fingers so she can pull it free from him, and all this time he hears the voice cracking and buzzing delightedly in his head.

'Kitten,' Aimee splutters. 'Oh my God, Kitten –'

Agatha is wrapping a tea-towel around his hand, which has begun to pour out blood. 'I'm sorry,' he gasps, 'I'm awfully sorry . . .'

The girl's beginning to fear you, Latch. Of late, you are always sour with her. You seem to despise her.

133 ⤙

No, no –

Soon, she'll start to despise you in return.

He turns to her, desperate. 'Aimee,' he says, 'I'm sorry –'

She reaches shaking hands to her face and, sobbing, covers her eyes so she does not have to see him.

That night he sleeps alone on the cracked leather couch in the lounge room. He thinks Aimee is pleased with this arrangement, because no one wants to lie beside someone who will deliberately impale his own palm. The wound makes him restless and vaguely feverish. He has fought off Agatha's efforts to take him to the doctor for antibiotics. He shies away from doctors, not wishing them to discover he is an untypical patient.

He lies awake into the night, huddled in blankets that give him no warmth. All his bravado is gone and he is afraid. He has never heard of an entity such as Paul. He has searched his intelligence, delving into all he knows of the ancient Legion for a clue, a similarity, something to give the voice truth and history, to make the connection between devil lore and human reality. He has held the malignant daemons up to the light, examining them like jewels: the Revenants, the returners, fearful and peevish, capable of inflicting physical harm: their existence is ghostly, they don't inhabit a breathing form. The Forso, the bored dead, exasperating when they reach their fingers into the business of the living but made content by a visit to the grave, a reassurance they have not been forgotten. The Inua, which weaves its way into a living host but is seemingly benevolent, for it produces no pain and places each captured soul in the heavens, as a star. Xenoglossia, tongue of a stranger, the demon's voice hissing through a body, but a demon that must be called in a complicated and magical way, which never arrives of its own accord. Taxim, a restless soul, always appearing as a shambling decaying corpse; vicious Preta, murderous to its relatives but, again, a ghostly thing. Nothing, nothing: Kitten feels himself floundering in all he does not know. It terrifies him, how defenceless he had been to resist the driving of the fork, the shouting of the words. He looks forward, and is appalled by what he sees.

If there ever was a natural parent then it has clearly forsaken him, and he feels this as a hard humiliation. Lying alone in the dark room he feels gutted, desolate. Paul has been silent for hours although Kitten feels the presence in the regular throbbing of his hand. With no natural parent and no relief in his knowledge, he is forced to look elsewhere for something that might help him. Closing his eyes, he steps into his head.

In his mind there are many rooms and no windows or doors. The floor is made of wood which is polished and gleams, reflecting his own image. The walls are white and reach into invisibility and it is dizzying to search for the ceiling. The rooms shimmer with a rainbow of oily colours that swirl about on the edge of his vision and vanish when he looks too closely. It is quiet, and he hears each footfall echo. For a long time he wanders about, searching for the twins. The twins had once consumed all the space in his mind but now he imagines them huddled in a corner, shivering as he shivers, clawing each other for comfort and warmth. He longs to lift them up and hold them, tuck them into the folds of his coat, carry them safely back to reality. He calls to them again and again. Come to me, my twins, I need you –

'Twins!' he calls. 'Twins!'

And the words slip off the polished walls and come sliding, unanswered, back to him. The pain in his hand jumps and jumps.

Later Agatha thinks she hears him, wandering through the house like a spirit haunting what it must leave behind. She hears his footsteps which she knows so well, circling the house from room to room. Lying in her bed, she wonders what he searches for, what damage has been done to him, how far he drifts from them. She is an old woman, but Kitten is older, there's ancientness in him, in his eyes there's the dustiness and clarity of centuries. She has never understood him and knows she never will, and that he does not expect this of her. They share the same world, but the space of infinity divides them. Not understanding him, she cannot help him. She may stand beside him, but she cannot touch him. Clasping her hands beneath the bed sheets, she mutters old prayers for him.

Kitten moves his blankets and pillows underground, to the pitch concrete confines of the bomb shelter. He makes a nest for himself in a dank corner, and in this bleak lonely place he sleeps comfortably.

FROM THE FRONT veranda Aimee watches Kitten. He is prowling the perimeter of his garden, following the shape of the horseshoe back and forth. For long minutes he is hidden from her and then he reappears from around the corner of the house. His pace is so even she can pick the exact moment she'll see him again. He's given no indication that he's noticed her but she's sure he must have, for nothing ever escapes him. He walks with his head bowed and he whispers continuously to himself. Now and then he lifts his hands from his sides and rubs them together or swings them into the air. He seems to be explaining some-thing, or re-enacting some event.

It is two days since he drove the fork into his palm and the thought of what he did to himself still makes her gag. Agatha had put a bandage around the wound but yesterday he had removed it and replaced it with a silk handkerchief which he tied very tight and plucks at, now and then, as he walks. He has not returned to Aimee's bed, evidently preferring the bomb shelter.

At the table he sits tight as a spring. He will not eat more than a few mouthfuls of a meal. He says nothing. He seems to listen, with a bird's intensity, to everything

Agatha and Aimee say, but if he is aware of how faltering and awkward their conversation is around him, he makes no comment upon it. Some times when he looks at Aimee his gaze is distant and blind; at others it is as if he can see her soul and all the working organs within her.

Yesterday he had spent hours in the garden but by the end of the day he had made little difference to it. He'd snapped off small branches, dug ditches in the earth with his fingernails. He'd pulled weeds but seemed to grow bored or forgetful in the task and left them grappling with the earth, their roots clinging to balls of soil. He had plucked petals from the flowers and scattered them across the ground. He'd left his precious tools out overnight, and the dew had settled and would make them rust. His silken bandage is filthy, but he will not take it off or wash the wound.

Aimee watches him disappear around the corner of the house. Beside her, the cockatoo shifts its footing and shakes its white feathers. It too has been watching him, and it's nervous and unsettled. It keeps one eye on the place where he vanished, waiting for him to fill it again. The wrongness of him swirls in the air, everywhere.

Kitten walks in the shadow of the house. His feet find the ground with certainty, but he sees nothing of what he passes. Inside his head, he flies through the vast and shining rooms.

Kitten, say you are without worth.

I will not.

Say you are no devil.

No, no.

Kitten, feel this.

He feels a small pain in his calf, like a splinter driving in.

Do you know what that is, Kitten? My fingers are in your muscles. I am pulling apart the fibres that make you. Say you are no devil.

. . . No.

Feel this, Kitten.

The pain in his leg grows sharper, deeper, and his pace falters.

Inside you, your feeble muscles spew blood. I am wounding you from inside. Say you have no purpose. Say it.

The pain is enough to make him stop. He concentrates his energy on defiance. He fights to be calm, to laugh. Pauly, you are a sad and loathsome aberration.

Feel this. Feel the barbs churn within you? Each touch from me adds misery to your life. Here: you will burn your flesh. Here: you will fall on stony ground. Here: a knife you hold will slip through a finger. Here: glass on the street will find your bare feet. Here: you tumble from a roof. Say you are without worth.

The agony in his leg races the length of his spine, making his shoulders hunch. I will not. I will not.

I am clouding your lungs. I am slowing your heart. I am thickening your veins. I am hollowing your bones. I am blackening your brain. I am making a happy home for plagues of many kinds. I am diseasing you, Kitten Latch.

Tears have come to Kitten's eyes, and he sways on his feet. I did nothing to you, Paul, nothing that didn't need to be done . . .

Each touch from me takes years off your life.

Kitten closes his eyes. His chest is tight and when he breathes, he sobs.

Say it. You are no devil. You are without worth.

Kitten paws at his tears, and slowly shakes his head.

Must the pain worsen, cur? Will I break your legs? Slice your throat?

. . . I am without worth.

You do not deserve the name devil.

I do not deserve devil.

You are just a boy.

Yes, yes . . . leave me . . .

A crazy boy with voices in his head.

A crazy boy with voices in his head.

You have lost.

Yes.

Good.

The voice leaves him, and Kitten opens his eyes. He is looking at the grass, and tears are dropping down his cheeks. I have lost: I have lost. He touches his aching legs, rubs the pain away from them. He apologises to himself for what he has done: he asks forgiveness from his limbs, his heart, his head, from all the whims and traits that make him who he is. He does not wish to be Kitten any more, this creature he has denied. In the warren of his mind he finds a corner and sits down, back to the wall, palms to the floor. He claims this room as his own, and leaves what is left to Paul. Slowly, carefully, he starts the walk back.

Aimee's perch is a rocking-chair and as it moves it creaks the floorboards, a sound at once eerie and comforting. Kitten rounds the building, following the path he has pressed out along the border of the garden. Beyond the garden is a stretch of grass that meets the leaning stakes of the front fence. Beyond this is the road. After this, wilderness. Aimee turns in the chair, looking around at the land. She has always thought it pretty, but for the first time she sees it is secluded. There's no other house for miles. The three of them are very alone, here.

'Kitten!' she calls, and he glances at her and away. She steps from her chair and crosses the lawn to intercept him. He steps neatly around her and continues his aimless, determined walk. She grabs his wrist to make him stop.

'Kitten,' she says, 'what's happened to you? What's wrong?'

He blinks at the place where her hand touches him, and veers away when she lets him go. His eyes are wet and his beautiful face looks haggard. 'Kitten's very busy,' he tells her. 'You must leave him be.'

'But what are you doing? You're doing nothing –'

'Aimee,' he says, 'it's very serious, please stay away.'

'What? What is serious?'

'Nothing you would understand. Go into the house and give me some peace.'

Aimee shakes her head. 'No,' she says. 'I won't. You're frightening me, Kitten, and you're frightening Agatha. Tell me what's happened and I can help –'

His eyes are empty when he looks at her, there's nothing in them, not even anger. 'You're very boring,' he says. 'You're very presumptuous. What makes you think you can make any difference? If Kitten cannot help himself, how could a scrap like you be of assistance? Everything is beyond you, Aimee, and nothing concerns you. Do not try to understand. The best you can do is pray you do not get hurt. Because that's likely, you see. It's likely you'll get hurt. Stay out of my way and stop testing my patience.'

'Oh, Kitten,' she says, 'this is not like you –'

He finds this amusing, and smiles like a wolf. 'Strange you should say that,' he replies. 'I doubt I'll ever be like I used to be. If I were you I'd give serious thought to leaving this place. Go, go on. I don't need you. I don't want you. I'm quite tired of your whining voice, your endless bawling. Spare me it. Go back to that idiot friend of yours.'

Aimee steps away from him. 'Kitten, you know I can't go back. I don't want to go back. I want everything to be the way it was –'

'I am gone from you!' he shouts, and thumps a foot against the earth. 'I don't belong to you any more – I never did! Leave me, before I hurt you! You mean nothing to me, you waste my time!'

She turns and runs from him, terrified. As she reaches the steps she hears him say, 'Aimee – Aimee, please –'

She hesitates, her hand finding a post of the veranda and holding tight to its solid warmth. When she looks at him she sees his hands are at his face, his fingers digging into his eyes. She walks back to him slowly, not trusting him. Fear grows quickly once it is planted, and she is afraid of him.

He does not lower his hands as he hears her approach. He has made a gigantic effort to return, and the voice is starting to rage. He thinks he hasn't much time to say what he wants to say, and already the pain is stirring in his limbs. 'Aimee,' he whispers, 'I'm drowning.'

'Kitten, tell me.'

'Don't listen to the things I say –'

Silence.

'Something is happening that I can't explain –'

Silence, I said!

'– and when I speak the words are not my own.'

I warn you, Latch. Must I become stronger still?

'Aimee, there's a blight in me. It drives me down and takes my place. I must fight it by myself, but I will fight it, and it will not win, and you must wait with me –'

Latch! Latch! I will not tell you again!

He grips her shoulders, suddenly urgent. 'Aimee,' he says, 'haven't I done everything I promised I would do? When you needed saving, wasn't I there to save you? I've never left you, Aimee, I've never lied to you, I'll never leave you alone. Think back, to how you remember me to be. I didn't frighten you then, did I? I was never cruel to you. Remember the times we have ridden our bikes? Remember the things we have seen? Remember how we came here and unpacked our things and walked around, remember how we planted this garden? Remember the first time we met? Remember me, Aimee? Remember Kitten?'

She stares into his eyes, not saying a thing. Kitten squeezes her shoulders, and makes a small panicked sound.

You won't drive away what is closest to me. You did that to yourself while you lived. You will not do it to me.

'I need you now, Aimee,' he says. 'I'm begging you, wait for me.'

Latch. There will be no peace for you.

Frightened and confused, Aimee hesitates. She sees the face she loves, hears the voice she knows, but she is afraid. Kitten looks exhausted, distraught, hopeless, destroyed, and she's afraid of what has done this to him. So she hesitates, and the hesitation is obvious to all.

You will not do this thing to me.

She hesitates. It is done.

Kitten lets his hands fall from Aimee's shoulders, resigned. The car pulls up on the roadside and they both look across at the sound. A man steps from the driver's seat and holds his arms out to them. Aimee stares, unbelieving.

'Why,' she says, 'it's Paul.'

IT WAS SO easy to find her, when once it had seemed so hard. He'd packed a bag and followed the road signs, it was as easy as that. The town is not remarkable, though he'd somehow expected it to be. It is tiny and plain: it is not a place for holiday-makers, nor a place where travellers stop to rest. There are no trees, everything is brown and bent bandy: summer is strong and lingers, here. The main street has wide strips of dust and gravel along its edges, carved up by spinning wheels. Many of the shops are vacant and have been so for years. Those that are occupied sag under sun and dereliction. There is a bakery, a milkbar, a hotel with an empty bench out the front. There are no people on the street. The milkbar stocks sweets he has not seen since his childhood, candy ponies on lollypop sticks, cylinders of bubble-gum as long as his arm. The man behind the counter knew her, the cheerful girl with the pretty blond hair, she was difficult to miss, appearing out of nowhere with a taciturn brother or friend, a matronly granny or aunt. The man had drawn a map: he delivered the paper to the house every morning, he knew the area well. 'Look,' he'd said, 'for a little brown house with a fancy garden, that's the place you want.'

She'd seemed impossible to find and here she is, alive and real, standing in a garden.

'Paul,' Aimee says, as she comes to him. 'Paul, what are you doing here, what are you doing?'

She runs to meet him, throws open the gate that divides them, flings herself into his arms. Until this moment she has not realised how much she misses him, her older brother, her only sibling. He lifts her off her feet and spins her in circles, laughing with joy. When he puts her down she clings to him, staring adoringly into his eyes.

'How did you find us?' she asks. 'What are you doing here?'

'I thought I'd come for a visit,' he says. 'See what's going on.'

'I can't believe it,' she breathes, and giggles, bouncing on her toes. 'I can't believe you're really here.'

'Here I am,' says Paul. He looks at the house, and at Kitten. 'Is this your beau?' he asks.

Aimee feels her heart sink: she shifts her eyes from her brother reluctantly. She takes Paul's hand and leads him along the path, and they stop before Kitten. He has made no move. His face is dry, the tears are gone.

'Kitten,' says Aimee, 'this is my brother, Paul. Paul, this is Kitten Latch.'

Kitten stares at him. Paul is a big man, much taller than Kitten, and it fills Kitten with a child's breathless vertigo, looking up at him. Paul thinks Kitten less substantial than he imagined, a small thing to wield such influence.

'Pleased to meet you.' Paul holds out a huge hand. 'I know a lot about you, I think.'

Kitten steps backwards and away. He stares up at the man, speechless. Aimee laughs uncomfortably.

'Come inside, Paul,' she says, and grips his sleeve. 'Come and meet Agatha. You've heard about her too, haven't you?'

'The one who cooks good food, you mean?'

Aimee is hurrying her brother to the front door. The cockatoo screeches and flaps its wings, dashing sideways along the railing. She pushes her brother into the house and glances back to see Kitten, white faced, standing where she left him.

Paul.

There is no answer.

Paul?

The silence in his head blows about like a breeze.

Answer me.

He waits. Nothing replies to him. The silence is clearing, letting in the noise of the birds and the grass and trees. These sounds mystify him at first, he does not recognise them to be what they are. For so long he has heard only the grinding buzz of the monster in his head, he has forgotten the tune of everything else. Sweat breaks out all over him as he begins to understand.

Paul! Return! Speak!

It seems ludicrous, begging the entity back, yet it is

the best thing that can be done. Kitten repeats the call over and over. Finally he says, This is not fair.

Paul has left, and Paul is real. This is not fair.

Kitten turns and runs across the land. He bounds through the grass, a thin, ill-clad creature running like an animal that finds itself in the open and in danger. Like an animal he heads for cover, he runs until he reaches the peppercorns by the creek. He darts amongst their scrawling branches, grips the highest one he can hold, swings himself up into the safety of the leaves. He crouches along a branch, his fingernails clawing the bark, his chest heaving with exertion and fright. Paul is real. Paul is back.

He looks across at the house. The sturdy building looks serene, standing in greenery and vegetables. He expects at any moment the windows to blow out, the roof to cave in, the walls to fold like cards. He readies himself to block his ears and shield his face. He whimpers, tense with distress. Kitten is a child again, terrorised by the despot, afraid for his life. Paul is real. Paul, who could shred with words or just a look. Who would let the moment of punishment hang until Kitten would pray for it to come and be gone. Who drained the worth from everything and everyone, who made Kitten feel such an unloved, unlovable, soiled and unwanted thing that he wondered why he had been born: Paul, who knew how to hit so it would not leave a bruise. Paul. Somehow he has managed to take on life again. Kitten, in his great age and wisdom, has never heard of such a thing. It is a thing against nature, a warping of the natural law, an insult to everything that lives and has lived. A dead man finds a voice, a voice takes on form, breathes in air, becomes real.

He watches the house for many minutes. Nothing happens to it, it stands secure. From inside comes the gust of a man's heavy laughter. Paul had always been calculating: it is his triumph, Kitten supposes, to return in a shape that Aimee would recognise and run to. How he must be laughing, to find Kitten so easily pushed so far, hiding in a tree like a beast. Clutching the branch with his aching wounded hand, Kitten feels the first rattle of indignation. I am Latch, Paul, who defeated you. Don't you dare to laugh at me.

What made Latch?

The question comes from nowhere, and Kitten pricks his ears. What made Latch?

The natural parent made Latch.

No – what made Latch? What made Latch?

Kitten is confused. He takes his eyes from the house and looks inside his mind. And sees, there, the old, familiar darkness. The cavernous jumble of rooms is gone. The devil's twins flex their prickling claws, curl their lips away from their teeth. Kitten hangs his head, weak with gratitude and relief. My twins, brilliant twins, hello. Kitten hugs the branch, rubs his cheek along its roughness. Twins, I have missed you, I've needed you, it's good to hear your voices again.

What made Latch?

Latch made Latch. Yes, Latch made Latch. Paul Latch brought Kitten to life and Kitten Latch brought Paul to life. Latch made Latch. Flesh made flesh made flesh. Kitten has always been flesh, but Paul is nothing but death in a shell. Kitten lifts his eyes and glares at the house. The twins are coiled in his head, purring with excitement. Remember who you are, Kitten. You are Latch. You are old as the heavens. You have seen the rise of empires and the fall of centuries. Your voice is thunder. Your power is without bounds. Nothing may defeat you.

Inside the house, Aimee and Agatha are in danger. Kitten drops to the ground and walks steadily across the earth. You have made a mistake, Paul. Flesh should have been your victory, but flesh is Latch's world, and now you are in it you can be driven out. Flesh dies: have you forgotten that so soon?

Kitten lets the screen door slam after him. At the table, Aimee is sitting beside Paul. She leans toward him, glowing with delight. Agatha is at the kitchen bench mixing a hasty batch of sultana scones. Kitten stops before Paul and points his tattered hand. Paul looks up at him, smiling.

'Fool,' snarls Kitten. 'You have made the most unwise move of all.'

Paul seems baffled, his smile starts to dip. He searches for words and finds nothing that suits. Kitten leans down and fixes him with gleaming eyes.

'You shouldn't have come here,' he says. 'You won't

win. You're going back to the place you were never supposed to leave.'

Paul hesitates. His gaze slips away from Kitten and darts around the room. Kitten snaps his fingers and Paul looks back at him.

'I am Latch,' whispers Kitten. 'Look at me, Paul. Remember Latch? I saw you out once and I'll see you out again. We will know, then, who may laugh. Ha ha.'

Paul stares. Aimee, appalled, burning with shame, gets from her chair and goes to him. 'Kitten,' she says, 'this is Paul. This is my brother Paul –'

Kitten smirks. The twins are grinding their teeth. 'Oh, I know who he is. We know each other very well indeed. Latch made Latch, yes?'

Agatha grabs his collar and leads him away and he lets himself be taken, laughing as he goes.

She pushes him into the lounge room and swings the door after them. Kitten is chuckling to himself; he spins about the room, falls against the walls, elated. 'Oh, Agatha,' he laughs, 'I've been idle too long, it shall be a pleasure to go to work again.'

'Kitten,' she hisses, 'what's the matter with you?'

'The matter with me, my angel? There's nothing the matter with me. The problem doesn't lie with me, as you can see.'

'Kitten, I wish you would see a doctor –'

'Forget the doctor!' he barks. 'There's nothing wrong with me! Must you be shown? Look!'

He yanks the handkerchief from his hand and slaps his palm on the table-top once, and then again. Agatha winces, screwing shut her eyes.

'I'm pure and whole again,' Kitten declares. 'The twins have come back to me. Have I ever told you of my twins, Agatha? My secret armour. I thought they had died, I thought Paul had murdered them, but they're back and they're fine. With the twins, we will not lose. You needn't fear anything, now. I feel the old strength in my bones.'

'Kitten,' moans the woman, 'what are you talking about?'

He sighs good-humouredly. 'Oh, Agatha, for an angel you are very dim. Listen, and I shall explain. Paul has returned. I don't know how, but that doesn't matter. He must be dealt with, that's all I need to know. You would think, wouldn't you, that something dead would have the good grace to stay dead?'

'Kitten, that man is not Paul Latch –'

'Agatha, is old age blinding you? Take care, my friend! Stay here in this room and don't come out. Leave him to me. I look forward to putting an end to him again.'

'Kitten,' she pleads, 'I don't understand what –'

He wheels about and strides across the room, stopping when he is very close to her. She smells the earth upon him, and the coldness of the shelter. He jabs a finger at her face and says, 'You do not need to understand. It's never been required of you to understand.

Do only as I say. Stay out of my way. I will not have you hindering me. My task must be done. If you step in my way, I will throw you aside.'

'Kitten, that man doesn't want to hurt us, he's come to visit his sister –'

He hoots contemptuously. 'That's what you think, is it? And no doubt Aimee thinks this, too?'

'Of course – he's her brother –'

Kitten shakes his head, rolls his eyes. 'Her brother,' he drawls. 'Doesn't it strike you as odd, Agatha, that she's never mentioned this so-called brother before?'

'But she has!' Agatha wails. 'She's mentioned him a hundred times and you have never listened! You never listen to a thing you don't want to hear!'

Kitten stares at her. His fist hovers dangerously close to her face. She sees him wrestling with what she's told him, struggling to seize what is true. For a moment he looks assailable, and in this moment she says, 'I don't know how much longer I can bear this, Kitten. For years I've tried to help you, but you don't want to be helped. You don't want to be pure and whole. You've never wanted to be that.'

He is not listening, she sees: the opportunity has been lost. Kitten has swung his reasoning away from her. She makes one last effort to catch him, but as he turns away the silk of his shirt pulls smoothly from her grip.

He goes to the door and trots swiftly down the hall and Agatha rushes after him. On the linoleum of the kitchen floor he slides to a halt. He is laughing. 'Aimee,' he says, 'who do you think that man is? That man sitting there – who is he?'

Aimee, agonised, groans, 'Oh Kitten, I told you, this is Paul –'

'This man,' says Kitten, 'is an obscenity returned from the grave. He has adopted a disguise to hide his identity. Do not be tricked by him. He wants to take you away from me. He wants to take me away from everything. If you believe what he says to you, his task will be easy. I know him, Aimee, I've known him forever. He has been plotting inside my head. He's revealed all his intentions to me. He told me he'd come, and here he is.'

'Kitten,' Paul says soothingly, 'I haven't been in your head. I don't want to take anything from you.'

'Aimee, tell him you know who he is, tell him you hate him, that you don't believe in him. If you tell him, you'll weaken him. Aimee, tell him.'

Aimee is crying. The situation is tortuous to her and she reverts to a child's defence of tears. 'I won't say that,' she weeps. 'I can't say that, Kitten –'

'Kitten –'

'Shut up!' Kitten screams at Paul. 'I've heard your voice long enough! Aimee, say the words!'

'Oh Kitten, why are you doing this –'

Paul gets to his feet and Kitten ducks away from him. He snatches up a carving knife and brandishes it at the man's chest. 'Kitten!' shrieks Agatha, and Aimee covers her eyes. Paul freezes at the point of the blade, and Kitten smiles.

'Be careful,' he warns. 'You could hurt me once, but not any more. You think it was clever to take on flesh, but flesh dies, Paul, flesh dies. Say you will leave. Say you are defeated and leave.'

Paul towers over him, very still. 'Kitten,' he says, 'put the knife down.'

'Say you will leave.'

'Kitten, put that knife down!'

'Agatha, be silent. Say you will leave.'

Paul steps carefully backwards. 'All right,' he agrees. 'I will leave.'

'Leave now. Vanish. I command you. Remember who I am.'

Paul nods, his gaze fixed on the knife. 'I'll go,' he says, 'but I don't want to leave Aimee and Agatha.'

'You will.'

'It's not safe for them here.'

'You are making me very angry, Paul. That has never been in your best interests.'

'Kitten, please put the knife down –'

'You're not well, Kitten. You're a danger to them and to yourself.'

'Aimee, do not listen. Do not believe what he says.'

Paul turns to the girl. 'Aimee,' he says, 'who do you believe?'

Tears are dribbling down Aimee's face. 'Kitten,' she mumbles, 'Paul is right, you are in trouble –'

'Agatha,' says Paul, 'who do you believe?'

'You, Paul,' answers the old woman.

Kitten stares at them, astonished. In his head, the twins thrash with fury.

'They're afraid of you, Kitten.'

'It's true, Kitten.'

'Tell him I'm not bad, Aimee.'

'Kitten, he's not –'

'Say I'm good.'

'He is good, he is –'

'I'm not your enemy, Kitten, I'm your friend. I want to help you.'

'Silence!' Kitten yelps. His voice quavers uneasily; he adjusts his grip on the knife. 'I don't want or need your help.'

'But we do,' sobs Aimee. 'We want his help. Don't we, Agatha? We want his help. We want Paul to stay with us. He's a good man, Kitten, he's a nice man. We want him to be with us.'

Kitten gazes at her. She stares back at him, tears dripping off her cheeks. They are strangers now, and inside themselves something falls away. He looks over his shoulder at Agatha. 'Is what she says true?' he asks.

He looks wretched standing there, and it breaks her heart to say, 'Yes, Kitten, it is. Put the knife down.'

Kitten's shoulders fall. He drops the knife and it speeds to the floor. He shifts his stance, dizzy with defeat. He looks at Paul and says quietly, 'You are good, Paul. You have always been good at the terrible things you do. You have beaten me. I thought I would win, but it seems I am wrong. Maybe I have always been wrong. About you, Agatha, and you, Aimee. I thought you were worthy and dependable, but it seems that you are not. You have left me. I will leave you. I'll walk away. I'll give you another chance, if you like, to change your minds.'

Agatha sways in the doorway and says nothing. Aimee says, 'Kitten, why are you forcing me to choose? Do you want to take everything from me? First Curtis, and now my family?'

Kitten watches her sadly. 'Stay, then,' he sighs. 'It doesn't matter. A devil walks alone. That's so, isn't it, Paul?'

He walks stiffly across the kitchen and out the back door. As he crosses the paddock the twins are howling at him, they say he's failed, they have wasted their time, they should never have returned. Renounced and exiled, he blocks his ears to them. Things are bad enough.

Night comes. Agatha stands at the window watching for him. The three of them are in the lounge room. They have lit a fire to comfort themselves. Paul has asked and asked again, trying to make them agree to leaving. He is shocked at finding his sister here, terrorised by Kitten, imprisoned in a washed-out town and a house that is not quaint, as she had claimed, but miserably shabby. He is disgusted at Agatha for inflicting this upon Aimee, who deserves better, who has always known better. 'Kitten's ill,' he declares. 'He's a danger to the pair of you, and to himself. God, Aimee, if I'd known he was like this I'd have come to find you sooner.'

'He's not like this,' Aimee answers dully. 'This is not how he is.'

'We cannot pack up and leave him,' says Agatha. 'We can't leave him to wander about alone.'

And yet she knows he has always wandered about alone: alone is how he's lived his life. The ways of the world were never his way. She had grieved for him when he was young and the children at school shied away from him, sensing his difference from themselves, and when he begged to stay at home she let him, because she could not bear the thought of him spending his lunchtimes by himself. In his teenage years he endured a thick, frustrated rage that would clench his fists, carve his skin, seem to make him spark with its strength. That no one seemed to care for him made him furious, he would burn with spitefulness, hating what he did not have. To survive, he toughened himself to his isolation, and encouraged in himself the characteristics that separated him from others, his wisdom, his mutinous mind. He found for himself a stronger reality, a reality that existed before people and things: he taught himself to love the earth, the animals, the air. This gave him peace: he could sit silent and unmoving for hours and nothing reached him then. In the silence Agatha would feel him leaving her. He no longer wished to share himself, as a child does; he did not want the embracing affection he had once craved. He was independent and mysterious, proud and volatile, random and distrustful. Certain types of people were drawn by these traits: they would hang around the house and around him for a week or a month or more. Reality never lives up to romance, however: Kitten was difficult to be near. All of them would disappear with time. Kitten didn't seem to care. He was alone, but defiant.

He adapted to the world by allowing himself to drift as far from it as he pleased. He shunned school, leaving it as soon as he could. He never held a proper, paying job. He never learned to drive a car. Television irritated him, as did any mention of religion. He rarely drank: to be drunk filled him with a thousand terrors. His life was solely his: he kept his secrets from her. He must have known that one day she would choose herself over him, no longer able to cope with the man he had become. A man: not a child with a child's worries and chances but a man, his chances hemmed, his worries turned to sharp-edged desperations. This, too, he knew: he had clung to a waif of a girl as if to a gift. She had been a promise for his future, proof that the years of alienation were not meant to last forever and had done him no harm. In this, as in everything, he was wrong.

Agatha puts a hand to the glass, feels the coolness of the night.

'True,' Paul is conceding. 'We'll wait for him. He'll

come back. He's got nowhere else to go. Then we'll have to catch him.'

Aimee hugs her knees. She knows Kitten is lost to her, and lost with him is the life she lives here. But she is not sad, as she had sworn she would be, were such a thing to happen. What she feels is disillusion, and a harsh annoyance at herself. Kitten: she'd pinned such hopes on him, building him a pedestal that reached into the sky. He'd showered her with a rain of pretty promises, none of which he'd kept. He hadn't given her freedom: he had put her in a cage. He'd used his temper as a weapon, against her, until she'd behaved as he preferred. Everything she'd run from has followed her here, and she's fallen for it once again: she's been an accessory, made to fit the space that required filling. Kitten Latch is no angel: Kitten Latch is a devil.

'Catch him,' she echoes. 'You won't just catch him.'

If she could catch him, she'd kill him.

'We'll catch him,' Paul assures her. 'This has to be done. You realise, the two of you, that it needs to be done?'

'Yes,' says Agatha, 'it needs to be done.'

'It needs to be done,' Aimee agrees.

'We'll go to bed,' plots Paul. 'Make everything seem normal. We don't want him thinking he's worried us.'

Beneath the window, tucked away from Agatha's view, Kitten crouches tight. His hearing has always been excellent: he hears the words rumble through the walls. The twins toss in his head, black as night, red as flame. He is damaged, the hits he has taken are hard, but he is not totally defeated. He too understands what must be done. The twins, ever reliable, have explained it all clearly. He curls up tighter and waits into the night and watches the stars as they brighten, one by one.

KITTEN IS IN a cathedral. The air is sharp and cold. He is lying on a sleek bed that has silver rungs along its sides. He is fastened to the bed by his ankles and his arms. He lifts his head to look around. He sees the wound in his hand has healed and cleanly vanished, and that he is dressed in a flimsy white smock. He gazes up at the vast and distant ceiling, which is painted with clouds. Curving to meet it are arches, pointing up to it are stone spires, rolling down from it are marble scrolls. Peaked windows line the walls, scattering coloured light across the slate floor. Under the windows, saintly figures are carved. There's music coming from some-where, ringing out the voice of angels.

A man and a woman are watching him. They too are dressed in white. The woman steps forward and speaks softly to him. 'Good morning,' she says.

She is a beautiful woman, the most beautiful he's ever seen. Her beauty takes his breath away, and he mutters shyly, 'Hello.'

'You've been asleep for a long time. Do you feel refreshed?'

He tries to shrug, but the straps pull his shoulders down.

'Are you chilled? Shall I give you a blanket?'

Kitten shakes his head. He feels in good condition, but he also feels vulnerable: he is reminded, for a moment, of a small boy marooned in a strange place, caught in the company of strangers. The woman watches the memory shiver through him, and touches his cheek. Her touch burns on his cold skin, heats him through to his bones.

'Don't be afraid, Kitten,' she says.

'I'm not afraid,' he tells her, and even his voice sounds unfamiliar. 'I know who you are.'

'Do you? Who are we?'

'I think you are the natural parents. Is that right?'

The man looks up and smiles. He's been flipping through a sheaf of papers that are scrawled with symbols and words. The woman and the man exchange glances and they smile at each other, pleased.

'It's a great honour to meet you,' Kitten says. 'I thought you had abandoned me.'

'No,' the woman answers, 'we didn't. Why would we?'

'. . . I broke the law. I did not want to walk alone.'

'That is understandable. It is painful, to walk alone.'

'You're not angry?'

'No. We will never be angry with you.'

'I am relieved.' Kitten gives a weak laugh.

'Tell us, Kitten, what do you remember?'

Kitten thinks. His arms and legs are uncomfortable, pressed close to the mattress as they are. 'I remember the fire,' he offers.

'You burned down your house.'

'Yes.'

'Why?'

Kitten flicks up an eyebrow. 'Surely you know. You must have known what was happening to me. You are the natural parents.'

'Tell us anyway. We want to hear it all, from you.'

Kitten sighs, and flexes his numb fingers. 'There seemed no alternative,' he says. 'You know that Paul Latch returned from the dead. That wasn't right. I knew, inside myself, what a wrong thing it was. Everything about him was wrong. He didn't know you. He claimed he was my penalty for breaking devil law, but he didn't know of you. He wasn't sent by you. He was unnatural, you see? It's not natural, for people to return from the dead and harass their devils. There was only one way to conquer him. Nature disposes of the unnatural.'

'Fire is natural.'

'Yes. The twins decided fire was best.'

'Tell us what happened.'

'You wish to hear the whole story? Well then, let me think. When the lights went off in the house, I went to the shed. There was petrol and oil in there, and I found a tin of turpentine. I also siphoned the petrol from Agatha's car. I worked quickly, there was no time for dallying. I was uncertain of what Paul was capable of doing, you see: I was worried he could still hear my thoughts. So I was neither as neat nor so elaborate as I might have liked to be, under other circumstances. I knew flesh was Paul's failing, for flesh has failings. His mind could travel through time and space: his flesh could not. I used my tools to barricade the windows and jam shut the doors. Wedges and hooks and blades, slotted in silently, allowing no escape. He was not going to flee, his flesh was staying where I wished it to stay. I doused the house with petrol and oil and turpentine, and then I put a match to it. It was very effective, that building was tinder dry. There was a tremendous hiss, I remember, as the air rushed from the wood. Within moments it was too hot to stand nearby, so I climbed a peppercorn and watched it burn from there. The night turned brilliant orange all around. From where I sat, I could feel the heat. I remember seeing Cocky fly away. I hope he flies forever.'

'And then?'

'Even from that distance, and over the noise of the flames, I could hear the activity inside the house. I heard shouts and squeals: I heard the roaring of Paul. What must he have thought, I wonder, to find himself defeated once again? The windows exploded as the flames reared up around them, it was the most fearsome of sounds, it sent the twins into peals of laughter. And, you know, I could smell things, too: it seemed I could smell all the food that had been eaten in the house, all the words that had been said, all the thoughts that had crossed our minds. I cannot explain it: it was as if I smelled the end of everything . . . I stayed in the peppercorn until people arrived, drawn by the fire. They hoped, no doubt, to extinguish it, but by then the house was beyond saving. I climbed from the tree and walked away. I crossed many paddocks and roads. In the morning I was given a lift in a truck and I was grateful, for I was exhausted. The rhythm lulled me, and I slept for a while. When it travelled in a direction I did not wish to go, I got down from the truck and continued walking. I walked for three days. I had nothing to eat. I had only one place to go. I went home. That little house, it was just the same as we left it. The garden was overgrown, the scent of disuse was there, but everything was the same. There's different people living in the house next door, Aimee's place. I could have made friends with them, I think, I watched them from the window, and they seemed very nice. But I was not given the chance. Your messengers came to collect me. They brought me here. Here I am.'

'That's an interesting story.'

Kitten smiles, bashful.

'What of Aimee and Agatha, Kitten?' asks the man.

'A devil walks alone. A devil can have no friend. A devil may not even have an angel, in the end. A devil's duty is binding and strong. It is greater than those who come and go. I had to remember who I am, and what is my duty.'

'Who are you?'

Kitten is silent for a moment. He looks the man up and down. 'I am the devil Latch,' he says.

'And what is your duty?'

'To follow those who must be followed. To watch the wicked. To be the punishing force. Justice: that is what I am.'

'Punishing. Is that what you were doing to Aimee and Agatha?'

'. . . No. They didn't need punishing. They hurt me, but a devil is above malice.'

'They hurt you?' asks the woman. 'How did they do that?'

Kitten hesitates. He tries to shift his feet, but the strapping holds him fast. He remembers the loss he felt as he waited out that last night, the bitterness that soaked through him, the muffled whispering of the twins. Agatha, the unfaithful angel. Her heart had never been in her task. She would never have come to him if her husband had not died and left her lonely: she had used Kitten like a toy, something to fill her empty life. Aimee, the deceiver. For her he'd sacrificed the things that made him strong, that she, in turn, would have strength when it was needed. He had been drained by all he gave her, and she had used his gift to crawl at the moment he needed her to stand. They had made him trust them. They had made him vulnerable. They had encouraged in him an innocence, and innocence is the thing of fools.

'You left them in the house with Paul,' prompts the woman. 'What had they done to you? You are frowning at the memory.'

'What they did to me is of no consequence,' Kitten replies. The natural parents are proving themselves somewhat tedious. 'What matters is what had been done to them. I am not at fault in any of this, you'll recall. I am not vindictive, as a devil may not be. I did what I judged most appropriate in the circumstances. That is all.'

'It was appropriate to let them die?'

'Think of it,' Kitten sighs. 'They were corrupted. Paul had fooled them easily: they believed he was someone he wasn't. I couldn't have mercy on them, because they believed in him. As soon as they believed, they were doomed. If they'd lived, what would have become of them? Paul had claimed them. They were his. He was an evil and cruel man while he lived. He became much crueller after he was dead, I assure you.'

'So you doused the house in petrol, and let the three of them burn?'

Kitten nods wearily. 'I believe so, yes. I trust I did the right thing. I was alone. I was tired and worn down. The twins were yelling in my head, I couldn't think clearly. I tried to do what was right to do. I am sorry, if I have disappointed you.'

The woman has a cloth, and she wipes it gently across his face. 'We are not disappointed,' she says.

The touch of the cloth calms him, and the melody of her voice makes him yawn.

'What is this place?' he asks.

'This is a place for you to rest.'

'Is it where you retire devils?'

'Worn down, tired devils, yes.'

'Then my task is over?'

'Yes, Kitten, it is. You needn't do anything, ever again.'

He nods slowly, and sighs. The woman has filled a syringe and she slips the needle into his arm. 'What's that for?' he asks.

'It will make you sleep.'

'Oh. I will be pleased to sleep, I think. It's very peaceful here. It's beautiful. You are beautiful too, you know, both of you.'

The man smiles, and the woman strokes his wrist. Kitten closes his eyes. There is a brief and faint crackling sound in his head, and he sleeps.

This is what they do to him: they open his head and drag out the twins, who writhe and scream and crash their teeth, clutching with their claws at the curve of Kitten's skull. When they are freed they are wrenched apart and their long arms lunge for each other, desperate for their old embrace. Denied, they twine like cats around the hands that hold them, shredding off layers of skin, enraged, spitting venom. Finally they are sent skidding across the slate floor where they lie, pawing weakly at the cold surface, their damp skins allowing them no hold. The natural parents step upon the small soft bodies until the whimpering twins are silent and dead.

When Kitten wakes up they tell him he's not a devil any more, he's just an ordinary boy. He is no longer called Kitten: now he is Christopher. He can sit in the sun, if he likes, and when he's stronger he can walk around the grounds. Kitten nods drowsily, taking this in. His head feels excavated, but not painful.

'I was a great devil,' he whispers. 'I was a great devil, though, wasn't I?'

'You were the greatest of the devils,' his natural parents reply. They do not tell him he failed in his last task, that Aimee was not sleeping peacefully that night, that she was alert enough to remember the bomb shelter, that ancient, concreted place. They don't tell him that she cowered there with her brother and the old woman, the three of them wrapped in the same blankets that had made Kitten's humble bed. The house burned above them, choked them and terrified them but never touched them, in the damp cold safety of the shelter. It is kind of the natural parents, not to tell him this. Kitten watches them walk away. There are other devils to be retired that day.

An ordinary boy: Christopher. Kitten sighs.

Well, it will not last forever.

ALSO BY SONYA HARTNETT

Sleeping Dogs

The Willows are a dysfunctional family, and when one of the five children befriends an outsider who wants to uncover their secrets, the family's world is blown apart . . . Another powerful and disturbing book from this talented young writer.

Winner of the 1996 Miles Franklin Inaugural Kathleen Mitchell Award
Winner of the 1996 Victorian Premier's Literary Award Shaeffer Pen Prize.
Honour Book in the 1996 CBC Awards.

Wilful Blue

In this haunting novel, Sonya Hartnett brilliantly explores the intertwined nature of talent and pain, and the mysterious and enduring bonds of friendship, love and memory.

Winner of the 1996

Black Foxes

In a tale of adventure and dire catastrophe, of enemies and strong friendships, of bloody revenge and lasting love, *Black Foxes* traces the extraordinary life of a young man who has everything and nothing, and who learns to live with it.

Princes

In a dilapidated mansion overrun by rats, Ravel and Indigo Kesby have gone to war. In this house, there's no such thing as brotherly love.

Looking for Alibrandi   Melina Marchetta

Josephine Alibrandi feels she has a lot to bear – the poor scholarship kid in a wealthy Catholic school, torn between two cultures, and born out of wedlock. This is her final year of school, the year of emancipation. A superb book.

Winner of the 1993 CBC Book of the Year Award for Older Readers.
Winner of the 1993 Kids' Own Australian Literary Award (KOALA).
Winner of the 1993 Variety Club Young People's Talking Book of the Year Award.
Winner of the 1993 Australian Multicultural Children's Literature Award.

Ganglands   Maureen McCarthy

The dramatic story of the summer when Kelly leaves school – when she will be faced with the toughest decisions of her life. Set in the cultural melting-pot of inner-city Melbourne, from the author of the *In Between* series.

Queen Kat, Carmel and St Jude Get a Life   Maureen McCarthy

A wonderfully passionate and absorbing novel about three very different girls in their first year out of school.

Shortlisted for the Victorian Premier's Literary Awards Shaeffer Pen Prize for Young Adult Fiction and the 1996 New South Wales State Literary Awards.

Sanctuary   Kate de Goldi

Months after a dramatic tragedy has brought her life to a standstill, Catriona Stuart is embarking on a painful search for the truth. The truth about her boyfriend Jeremiah, and his dangerous brother Simeon. About her wayward mother Stella. About her past. And, most of all, about herself, and her secret, and why her world fell apart.

Obernewtyn   Isobelle Carmody

In a post-apocalypse world, Elspeth is one of a new breed of mind thinkers and seeks the truth of her strange powers. A search inevitably leads to the sinister and mysterious Obernewtyn.

Book One in the Obernewtyn Chronicles. Shortlisted in the 1988 CBC Book of the Year Awards.

The Farseekers   Isobelle Carmody

Their refuge, Obernewtyn, is under threat. Only Elspeth and her allies have any hope of resisting the forces of evil. And time is running out.

Book Two in the Obernewtyn Chronicles. Named an Honour Book in the 1991 CBC Book of the Year Awards for Older Readers.

Ashling   Isobelle Carmody

Elspeth's old enemy Ariel is back and is seeking revenge, and she herself must finally confront her feelings for Rushton . . . an unputdownable read.

Book Three in the Obernewtyn Chronicles.

Darkfall   Isobelle Carmody

Glynn and Ember are 16-year-old twins on holiday in Greece, when they are transported to the mysterious world of Keltor – a world that is full of dissent. What is the mysterious connection between Glynn's world and Keltor? And why does the man who rescued her from the waves bear an eerie resemblance to Wind, her beloved instructor.

Darkfall marks the beginning of a stunning new trilogy from one of Australia's leading writers of fantasy.